DARKEST DAY

JOSEPH D. NEWCOMER

DEAD
STAR
PRESS

ACKNOWLEDGMENTS

&

DEDICATIONS

For parents—those who would be if they could be, those who aren't or choose not to be, those who are, even though they couldn't be, and those who do it alone.

All of it is life, and none of it is easy.

&

My Family

Andrea Greenwald & Ariella Nova Newcomer

Thank you for your support,

William Hetrick, Aron Shaffer, Zack Colman, Lee Edmondson, David Johnson, DAJO, TJ, The Ottenas, Trevor Huster, Jared White, Zachary Short, Sperry Hutchinson, Sebastien Reyes, Stuart Shoen, Katie Turk, The Trohoskes, Greenwalds, Turkos, McCalls, Ciminos, Colemans, Wokutches, Sousaes, Pitkins, Bruinsmas, Kuligowskis, Wards, Carl Michael, Corban Ford, Adonnis Blake, Andrew Dady, Sylvia & David Newcomer.

1. Suburban Decay

A plague of crushing dread clamps his throat the instant his hand touches the doorknob. Tom will be out there, and, of course, he'll be radiating obnoxiousness in the picture-perfect, suburban-morning sunlight. It was worse before, but this is still the worst part of Chris's day. It is also the most comforting and familiar part. Two years have given him enough time to stop comparing his life to the way it used to be. He's aware of how much easier everything seems, but it no longer affects how he feels every moment of the day.

The glossy red paint on the door snaps away from the sticky, rubber weather stripping. Chris prays he is wrong as he peeks out of the opening. The door only cracks slightly, and Tom is already waving and smiling like an asshole from the neighboring lawn. The scene continues in agonizing slow motion, but Chris cannot turn away. The Sun glares off all three hundred of Tom's enormous, painted-on, white cartoon teeth as they threaten to jump out of his preposterously giant mouth. In an L.S.D. trip-inspired, toothpaste commercial nightmare, Tom's garish dental anomalies skip across the driveway, surround Chris, and shout repetitive, singsong taunts of, *"We're better than you are. We're better than you are."*

"Hey, bro!" Tom shouts from his yard.

"Oh, hey, Tom."

Chris wrings his guts for an ounce of cordial tone while his shoulders defeatedly fall away from his neck. He pulls the door closed softly, and he carefully locks the deadbolt. In his mind, the waking nightmare fades as Tom's teeth run off into the neighboring yards to find more unsuspecting victims to terrorize and belittle. Tom stays behind, to the strangling dismay of Chris.

"What the fuck, man? What are you sneaking around for?" Tom continues to shout from his yard.

"Just trying not to wake up Cece."

Chris walks down his steps and turns toward his car away from Tom, hoping this will cut short any further conversation.

"Whatever, it's already eight o'clock. Dude! Did you watch that fucking game last—"

Chris's thoughts cut off Tom in mid-sentence. Tom's words are reduced to muffled, incoherent mumbles under Chris's mental lamentations, *"God, I hate this motherfucker. Please, just one, give me one goddamn morning without this asshole. Just one fucking morning!"*

Tom moves to the next subject without hesitation or a need for a response as he turns toward Chris and steps over the short, brick wall separating their front yards. Chris pauses and looks back to see Tom tossing a baseball over his shoulder to a small crying boy in an oversized Pittsburgh Pirates cap.

"Practice your throwing stance."

The ball dribbles through the thick grass to the child's feet. Chris looks around his quickly approaching neighbor at the bawling child throwing his glove on the ground. The boy falls to the lawn with his arms and legs crossed, and he continues to pout.

"Kid's gonna be the next Andy Van-fucking-Slyke," Tom boasts as he hustles to catch up to Chris.

Tom steps into Chris's path, trapping him into interacting.

"Really? He doesn't look like he's having any fun at all." Chris turns to look at the boy again. He nods to direct Tom's attention to the boy as well. "Jesus, Tom! He actually looks miserable."

For a moment, both men watch the howling child as he rips handfuls of grass from the lawn and throws them in frustration.

"Ah, ya gotta let 'em cry it out sometimes. He'll toughen up. Anyway, are you guys ready for the big party? That little shit's only gonna turn seven once, ya know? We rented a bounce house with a slide to the pool. We have floating platforms and American Gladiator-style jousting sticks so that those crazy little fuckers can beat the shit out of each other. Three fucking kegs!"

"Kegs?"

"Of course, man! Booze too, I mean, if you're too good for beer, fancy boy?"

Chris winces at Tom's aggressive car salesman laugh. The throaty guffaw buzzes and distorts in Chris's ear while his ribs are prodded by Tom's elbow.

"What a fucking asshole!" Chris's internal voice takes over his perception again, but more polite words fall out of his reluctant grimace.

"Yeah, I mean, we plan to be there," Chris responds, inching past Tom, away from the conversation, and closer to the car.

They've had some variation of this conversation several times in the past two weeks. Chris is lost as to why he is continually asked the same question and why he must, once again, give the same answer. Tom is transparent and annoying but harmless. It's apparent that he gives so little of a shit about their actual interactions that he can't even remember the crap that came out of his mouth the last time he felt the need to harass Chris with his boorish presence. In

3

Chris's estimation, Tom's incessant repetition must be due to either his uncanny self-involvement or his explicit need to have something to say every time another warm human body is regrettably within earshot. It crosses Chris's mind that it just may be a little of both.

He manages to get around Tom's alpha body, but not far enough away from its omega mind. Chris opens his driver's side door. Silently and futilely, he begs fate, once again, to end the conversation. He tosses his shoulder bag through the door and onto the passenger seat as he slides into the driver's seat and starts the hesitant engine of his late-nineties Corolla. To Chris's amazement, as it is every day, the two-hundred-thousand-mile-plus-motor clacks over the whining starter until it stutters to a fumbling idle. Tom knocks on the window and mimes an exaggerated roll-down motion with his hand, obviously mocking the fact that the car does not have automatic windows. His every expression is in perfect step with his insulting bravado. Leaning across the front seat, Chris wrestles the window down. As the glass whines against the worn rubber trim, Tom chuckles.

The knob jams, leaving a quarter of the window unevenly sticking up in the window frame. This is as far as the window has been able to roll down for years.

"Dude! This thing's a dinosaur. Get a new car already." Tom leans his head into the car and lowers his voice. "Listen, I wanted to ask you, you all right, man? You seem worse than normal. My sister giving you a hard time? You look like fucked shit, brother."

Chris's breakfast curdles in his abdomen. This familiar stomach-turning reaction happens each time Tom calls him *brother*. Chris slips into another daydream of slowly rolling up the screeching window into Tom's fist-sized Adam's apple. As the edge of the glass meets Tom's throat, Chris fights the alluringly homicidal mental vision and tries to respond.

"Yeah, no, everything is fine, man."

4

"You guys still trying to pop one out?" Tom launches into a new line of intrusive questioning.

Shuddering with contempt, Chris closes his eyes and shakes his head. The daydream persists. Chris pulls more forcefully on the window crank, and the glass pinches clean through Tom's neck. Cartilage and muscle pop and crack until Tom's severed, but somehow bloodless, head falls into the passenger seat and onto Chris's shoulder bag. Staring up at Chris, the disembodied head continues speaking without skipping a beat as though it is completely unaffected. The neck stump of the headless body squeaks as it drags against the passenger door window on the way to the ground outside of the Corolla.

Tom continues with no regard for any sort of decency, boundaries, or awareness of Chris's now outward disgust for the decapitated head in the passenger seat, "They said on the news they got those pesticides in everything, and that's what's fucking everybody up. Christ, you can't even eat cereal anymore. Guess we're lucky we're done having those little bastards. Five is enough. With Cynthia about to go into her terrible twos, I'm done spreading my seeds. You know what I mean? The other day, they said the same chemicals are in all those antidepressants too. Everybody wants to be happy. No one can accept that you just can't be happy all the fucking time. Life ain't all BJs and boner pills. Hell, I guess we don't have anyone to blame but ourselves."

Chris shakes the disturbing vision of Tom's bodiless head and looks up to find him entirely intact, still leaning into the car.

"Jesus Christ, Tom!" Chris is repulsed, but he isn't shocked. This is all part of Tom's crass and tiresome but expected routine.

"What? I'm not making this shit up. Don't get mad at me. I mean, it's not just you. Lots of guys' jizz is on the fritz. Hey, speaking of boner pills, you know, you do need to make sure she's having a good time, too, even if you guys can't get pregnant. Truth be told, I have some potent shit me and the wife use if you ever—"

Chris unsuccessfully begs his mind not to succumb to picturing Tom taking "boner pills" and any of the disgusting, sordid exploits up to, and including, the "BJs" that might happen afterward. He clunks the shifter into reverse, interrupting Tom. The car jumps and begins to roll down the driveway.

"Bye, Tom."

Tom is pulled alongside the car for a step before letting go of the window ledge. He waves and shouts while Chris backs down the driveway.

"Later, bro! Just say the word if you need some. No judgment here, dude."

The front tire of the Corolla jumps the curb. Its worn springs, shocks, and struts whine and clank like an overused bed in an old west brothel as the car bounds onto the road.

2. O.K. Package

"Hey, Chris."

The forced whisper coming over the cubicle unlocks Chris's attention from the coffee stain on his cubicle wall. Chris didn't make the stain. He doesn't drink coffee. It was probably there for years before he started sitting here, but Chris isn't considering who was responsible for the mark. He isn't thinking about how it got there or the mundane exchanges and trite office interactions that led to the fumbling of a cup, which, in turn, made the hideous, sleazy hotel sheet-looking stain. It was merely in his eyeline. The stain stared back at him for the past half-hour while he tried to decide how long he would have to sit at his desk before he could leave for an early lunch, how early he could leave without anyone questioning him about it, and what he would have to do to keep from having to talk to anyone about anything.

He had decided on eleven forty-three. It was close enough to noon that, when speaking about it, a person would have to reference noon instead of eleven. If the VP of sales came out and asked Kent where his cubicle neighbor was and how long ago he left, Kent would nervously and, no doubt, annoyingly say, "Ah, um, I think he went to lunch, it was ah, like a quarter to twelve." He certainly wouldn't say eleven forty-three. No, not even that pitiful, squeaky, raw taint of a human being would be that shitty and exacting. There's office code to consider. If it's not your responsibility to know, and it can fuck up someone else's world, when a superior asks a question, the answer is you're not a hundred percent sure. As a result of this unspoken rule, most answers in a corporate setting are divinely vague and include prepositions like *about* or *around* and phrases such as, *"Let me check into it,"* or, *"I'll have to get back to you on that."*

Chris is fully aware that the only thing more important to Kent than physically shoving his nose into the assholes of every person in a higher position than himself in the office food chain is his desperate need to be liked by his coworkers—by people in general. His conflicting hopes for popularity and advancement render him nearly entirely useless. His penchant for openly singing female pop songs while wearing his headphones in the break room doesn't do much for him either. He is oblivious to his volume and, even more so, to the less than desirable tone of his perpetually sharp falsetto.

Chris can sense Kent twitching back and forth in the cubicle next to his. He can hear his feeble co-worker fretting and mulling over his indecisions and apologizing to every person on the phone and every person in the office for absolutely fucking everything—for absolutely fucking nothing. The truth is that no one dislikes Kent, not even Chris, but it doesn't matter. Kent is not the kind of person who can allow himself to be accepted by others enough to reach a level of comfort that might afford him the opportunity to make a "real" friend.

The same lack of confidence that keeps Kent on the fringes of any social group also keeps him from realizing his worth at his worthless job. He's not a rat, though. He's just incapable of improvisation. So, eleven forty-three is close enough to be rounded to a quarter to twelve without Kent feeling so guilty about lying that he would beat himself up over it, or worse yet, say eleven forty-three, which sounds a lot more like eleven thirty than noon. These are the thoughts that occupied Chris's attention while he stared at the coffee stain on his cubicle wall until now, eleven thirty-three, as he is startled by Decker peeking over his cubicle wall, opposite Kent's half-audible apologies and paper shuffling. Chris instinctively grabs a pen and pretends to be writing until he realizes that it's Decker looking at him. He drops his pen, relaxes, and turns to Decker.

"We gotta cut outta here, man! I need a drink or something."

Chris scans the area to check if anyone is nearby enough to listen in on their conversation.

He turns back and whispers, "A drink, again? It's not even lunchtime, man!"

"C'mon, Chris! I just saw Jackhole go into the shitter with his phone. He's good for at least half an hour in there, and then he's going to lunch. Besides, he hasn't freaked out on anyone since Darkest Day. We're all good until at least one o'clock."

Jack Holt is the Executive Vice President of Sales at O.K. Package. Holt is also a complete dickhead, but Decker is right. Chris hasn't seen Holt be remotely rude to anyone, not even Kent, for the little over two years since Darkest Day. Even though old Jackhole's behavior had drastically changed in the past two years, after ten years of dealing with his absurd dickheadedness, it was difficult to let it go. After all, this was the same man who, a few years earlier, tried to make it an office policy that employees could only use the restroom while on their lunch breaks. Luckily, Legal caught wind of it, forced Holt to recant his shouted, expletive-riddled announcement, and issue an apology to the entire staff.

Kent still only takes dumps on his own time, but after almost two years of old Jackhole not tearing anyone a new place from which to take a dump, Kent has finally started sneaking away to relieve himself on company time—number one only. He is still quick about it and completely discrete, except for whispering to Chris to cover for him, to which Chris generally replies, "Kent, just go to the fucking bathroom, man!"

Chris and Decker pause as Paula, the Chief of Operations, struts in front of them. Her neck nearly breaks as she gawks and bats her eyes at Decker while she passes. Chris is uncomfortable. He finds her overt public display of humiliating high school crush to be repugnant. Listening to her speak was always demoralizing for Chris. Everything about her is a put-on—her designer knock-off pantsuits, her dyed-blond hair with dark roots, her painted-on smile, but it's her contrived and absurdly high-pitched voice that carves into the base of his skull. It's like a shiv fashioned from a spoon, gouging into a concrete wall, etching the number of days he's spent in this prison cell of an office. She ends each office interaction with shrill clichés and rhymes—*"Catcha later, alligator!"*—*"Awesome blossom!"*—*"See ya on the flip side!"* Each time her words scrape down his ear canals, Chris's dick shrivels with revulsion as it desperately tries to climb inside of his own body. He had already overheard her exclaim, *"Okie Dokie, Artichokie!"* earlier today, and that was about all the more he could withstand.

The entire ordeal of Paula is infinitely worsened by Decker's insistence on reveling in her obvious fantasy. She had always been punishing enough alone, but with her new crush, Decker, egging her on, Chris is reaching previously unimaginable heights of irritation. She isn't an unattractive woman. She's actually quite lovely, but Chris cannot get far enough past the treachery of her fabricated workplace existence to find a human who could exist outside of the fluorescent bulb-lit, neutral-colored walls of O.K. Package. He wonders if this persona does stop outside of the glass doors. He can't fathom that she'd be this way in her personal life or why anyone would choose to act like this any of the time, but he also cannot imagine her being any different. His stomach acid bubbles into his throat, anticipating her blaring voice alarm.

"Hey, Decker, how are you?" She flaps her tar-dipped, impossibly long, fake eyelashes and meekly waves with a flourish of her fingers.

"Oh, hey, Paula! Lovely to see you. Have a lovely day!" Decker responds with excessive warmth, which only exacerbates the boiling of the acid in Chris's belly.

"You first!" she manages to draw out the word "fir-irst" into two syllables with all the bleeding-eared, cheery playfulness of a nursery rhyme whistled through a poorly played toy recorder.

Decker mirrors her coy wave back at her. Turning the corner, she smiles and waves again.

"Dude, you're fucking married!" Chris's upper lip arches in disgust, baring his teeth.

"What? I just said, 'Hello!'"

"Yeah, I heard. It was lovely," Chris exaggerates Decker's gushing tone.

"Dude, do you want to cut out of here or not?" Decker asks again.

Decker's whisper stirs Kent. His jittery squirrel head pops up over the opposite wall. Chris and Decker silently stare at him until his skittish glances around the office land on them.

"Oh, hey, guys." Kent's volume registers just above a library voice.

Chris reluctantly forces a greeting, "Hey, Kent. How's it going?"

Rolling his eyes, Decker half-waves a couple of fingers with his hand limply hanging over the wall into Chris's cube. The lack of effort he put into the wave perfectly corresponds with the lack of expression on his face.

"Man! Yeah... pretty horrible, man!" the words spill out of Kent. He's obviously been dying to share his exasperation with anyone, and Chris's innocuous small talk released him to unburden his soul.

Chris silently begs himself not to ask, but his empathy overrides his selfishness as one of Kent's eyes involuntarily twitch and half-close.

"Why?" Chris asks.

"I almost fell in the shower last week!" The bulge of Kent's eyes, his otherwise plain face, and his tone beg, *Can you believe it?* as if there is no chance that Chris and Decker could respond with anything less than the total shock and sympathy Kent believes the situation rightfully deserves.

Pinching the bridge of his nose, Chris winces at the pain of trying to comprehend Kent's statement. "What?" he asks softly, repressing the urge to ignore Kent altogether and pretend he said nothing.

Decker pushes himself off the cubicle wall and crosses his arms over his chest. "You're horrible because you almost fell? In the shower? A week ago?"

Shuddering at the volume of Decker's voice, Kent whispers more quietly in an attempt at bringing the intensity of the conversation back down to a level that doesn't make him uncomfortable, "Yeah! I could have died!"

Decker's arms unfold, and he grabs the top of the wall. "So, you're saying that something that didn't actually even happen a fucking week ago is ruining your day"—he lets go of the top of the wall and taps on it to accent each syllable of the final word of his question—"today?"

Kent's chin recedes into his face and shoulders. "It was unsettling," he whimpers.

From the physical middle of the conversation, Chris stares straight ahead, no longer directing his attention at Kent or Decker as they speak. He presses his hands against his face and grinds his cool fingertips into his closed eyes.

Overly dramatic sarcasm pulls Decker's eyelids farther apart. "Sure! I mean, that must've been very traumatic for you."

Realizing the lack of sincerity in Decker's voice, Kent lowers his head and directs his words at himself, "It was." He shrinks away from the conversation and glances through his shame at Decker.

Decker flashes a merciless, plastic smile and stares directly into Kent's eyes. Kent desperately attempts to look in any other direction.

"All right. I'm done talking to you. Bye, bye." Decker flaps his fingers quickly twice, shooing Kent away from the conversation. "You can sit down now."

Kent continues to twitch while slowly looking away and sinking into his cubicle.

Under his breath, but loudly enough for them to hear him, Decker mimics Kent's whispering voice, "You fucking lunatic."

Decker slowly waves until Kent completely vanishes.

Kent's isn't the only psyche damaged by years of workplace supervisory guilt-shaming and micromanagement. Kent was, however, rendered ineffectual, almost subhuman, whereas Chris's conditioned anxieties aren't entirely debilitating. Occasionally, Chris still falls victim to the latent, passive-aggressive finger-shaking of corporate policy and culture, but he retains enough ambivalence or self-value to push through his guilt and break the rules if he thinks he can get away with it. He only rebels enough that it won't cause a situation wherein he'll be forced to spend an extended amount of time explaining himself if someone does happen to question him on it. He does his best to avoid lengthy conversations with anyone at the office, with the only exception being Decker. Decker doesn't seem to give a damn at all, but Chris is sure Decker suffers from the tug of trained attrition, even if he hides it better than anyone else. As the post-Darkest Day conversations of penitence become fewer and shorter, Chris is increasingly more apt to stretch the constructs of acceptable behavior with Decker.

"C'mon, man! Let's go," Decker pleads.

Chris's fingers are now pressed into his temples, kneading at what he's sure is about to be a migraine. His hands fall away from his head and push against his desk, sending his chair rolling away from the coffee stain and all the work he's been avoiding, the work he most likely would have continued to avoid for the remainder of the day, regardless of whether he stayed or not. He was already planning to leave before Decker started prodding him. Chris had planned on coming back to work, though. He's aware that if they go to the bar, they won't be back today, but he can't find the strength to care, knowing there won't be much of a punishment beyond the dreaded long conversation with Jackhole if they get caught. He checks the clock. It's eleven forty-two.

"Fuck it! Let's go."

3. The Last Fertility Doctor

They had agreed that their last visit would be their final attempt to find a fertility doctor who might have better news than the several they had already seen. They were given the same news with every new doctor, with every new test, with every admittedly low probability attempt at any type of fertilization. Yet somehow, each new result was just as, or more, gutting than the last for Cecilia. These let-downs—these empathetic sorries and shaking heads have stacked up on the sturdy back of Cecilia's soul, but it's clear to Chris that she can no longer bear their weight. Finally accepting the fate described to her ad nauseam for the better part of the last two years, she shut herself in the house for fourteen days straight, using more than half of her closely guarded personal days from work. She had saved a wealth of personal, sick, and vacation days in the hopes of having extra maternity leave. Chris knew then that it was overly optimistic at best.

Since their final visit two weeks ago, Cecilia and Chris have barely spoken. She barely said a word to the doctor when they were there. She didn't even have any questions. There were no more questions to be asked. Chris knew she'd been pushed beyond the limits of her strength, optimism, and will.

.   .   .

"While I realize that in my initial assessment, I was candid about the low probability of success, it still pains me to give you this news."

She had given them a three percent chance of successful fertilization. Carrying the child to term was substantially less likely. Still, these were the best odds they'd been given in a while. Her fingers interlace as her hands come together and rest apologetically on top of Cecilia's file on the desk between them. Crow's feet prematurely fan out from the corners of the young doctor's eyes. The rest of her face appears to be in its mid to late thirties at the oldest, but Chris can see that her eyes are far more mature. They are the thoughtful, honest, and tormented eyes of a person who has seen the greatest depths of human suffering. This is the same regretful speech they heard dozens of times. He prepares himself for the *"Sorry, but we are unable to help,"* to be inevitably followed by a compassionate and lengthy diatribe of all the reasons procreating may have become so difficult for so many people since the events of Darkest Day.

"Unfortunately, we were unable to fertilize any of the harvested ova."

The distant look in Cecilia's eyes grows as Chris turns to read her reaction. Her eyes turn down, looking at nothing. A blank stare replaces the faint glint of hope in her expression. There is a sense of relief in Chris that this will bring some finality to it—that now, maybe Cecilia will be able to begin to move on and heal. His feeling of solace quickly vanishes as he's overcome with shame for allowing himself any relief at all.

"At this point, there is nothing more we can do. I am terribly sorry."

This is the moment of silence before the explanation of how increasingly common their situation is. These quiet seconds are the most painful for Chris, and he assumes they are the same for Cecilia. He wishes he could cut off the obviously sweet and caring doctor at this point, but he won't. Maybe this is as cathartic for the doctors as they wrongfully believe it to be for the patients.

"Please understand that in today's environment, it is actually quite astounding that anyone is still able to have children naturally. The success rate of any type of medically assisted fertility is increasingly slim. You shouldn't feel alone. At this point, more than eighty percent of the population suffers from infertility. I assure you, that number is much higher than we know, but this is all we can say with any certainty, as not everyone has been tested.

"I can tell you for certain that the success rate in this office has been very low for the past two years, and once again, as I mentioned in your first visit, there hasn't been a single successful pregnancy in the past year. Our shortsighted use of compounds found in herbicides, pesticides, and many other everyday products has introduced a multitude of sterility-causing chemicals into our environment—Hexachlorocyclohexane, polychlorinated biphenyl, dichlorodiphenyltrichloroethane, tetrachloroethylene.

"Like I mentioned early on, to be perfectly honest, as a fertility doctor these days, I spend most of my time researching, not practicing. That's what anyone left in this field has been doing for over a year now. We're looking into the causes and trying to find more answers. Right now, there is a growing theory that some of the sterility-causing chemicals we once used, like the glyphosates still found in basically all our water and soil, have become more aggressive due to being irradiated by the widespread nuclear fallout resulting from Darkest Day.

"I understand none of this makes any of it better for you, but perhaps the knowledge that you're not alone can provide you some comfort."

The rigid, aging lines reaching from the outside corner of the doctor's modestly mascara-edged eyes soften as she settles into the familiarity of the speech she is so obviously accustomed to giving.

Chris senses the guilt in her voice tempering with the analytical de-tachment of explaining the more factual, less subjective information. The creases intensify when she comes to the more emotionally driv-en language.

Every word of this has been heard too many times. From what Chris could tell, each time Cecilia heard one of these speeches, she either blocked it out with her admirable and incredible strength of stubborn will, or she simply was physically unable to listen to anything they said after the word, *sorry*. He tried to be optimistic for Cecilia for a long time. He was supportive to a fault. Ever since they started trying to get pregnant, it was nearly impossible for Chris to be any other way. Whenever she had any trace of hope reluctantly light up her face, his gut instinct was to root for her. At this point, he can't, in good conscience, encourage her hope. In his mind, his false positivity is worse for her than his guarded apprehension. He thinks she must realize any enthusiasm he could project would be a lie by now. When he considers all the options for how he can best support her, when he is honest with himself, he can't imagine anything that he could do that would truly make it any worse or any better.

What could Chris say? What could the doctor say, for that matter? What did they know about how any of this felt for her? He knew the answer was that there was nothing he could say, nothing anyone could say. Chris knew he could never truly understand how she felt. He could only hope that she'd come to terms with it at some point and that the space and quiet he would allow her would be what she wanted. This may not be the best way, but it is the only way he thinks he will be of any use to her.

He was relieved when she decided this would be the last time they would try. This, he knew by definition, was insanity, and he couldn't bear to witness her go through this process again. In the un-utterable words of his conscience, he prays Cecilia is connecting with any part of what the doctor is saying, but it is clear from watching her stare with the vacuous eyes of a cadaver at the doctor, she is not.

"I would also be happy to refer you to several wonderful therapists I know personally and highly recommend. As I'm sure you are aware, this can be a difficult time, emotionally, for anyone. You can't overestimate the importance of having the guidance of someone qualified to counsel you, someone with quantifiable experience with these highly delicate matters. That goes for you as well, Mr. Adams. We could all benefit from a little therapy. Please, don't hesitate to reach out to us if either of you should need anything at all."

The doctor hands Chris a pamphlet. He leans over the desk to take it, knowing he will not read it, knowing he probably should.

"Thank you," Cecilia says, barely above the volume of a funeral conversation, her voice abandoning all emotion.

She stands abruptly. There are no tears. She is well beyond that type of outward show of sadness. There are no questions. Every question has been answered more times than any human could ever need to hear. Without hesitation or a look of confirmation to Chris, she decisively turns, walks quietly around her chair, and leaves the room. Chris jumps out of his seat, startled by Cecilia's quick exit.

"Thanks. Thank you," he rushes his words and fumbles over them as he tries to leave quickly and catch up with Cecilia. "We really appreciate everything you've done. Thanks. Uh... thanks." He skittishly places the pamphlet on the credenza next to the door while he awkwardly backs out of the room. "Thank you."

4. The Miracle Dick

"I almost never masturbate standing up. Or, really, when I'm lying down either. Do you think it's more likely that sitting down makes me want to masturbate or that thinking of masturbating makes me want to sit down?"

It's evident by his exaggerated facial expressions that Decker is actually considering the answers to his questions. Chris is not entertained by Decker. Even if he were, he wouldn't let on that he found these absurd and generally repulsive, esoteric ruminations of Decker's amusing. Chris would never dream of encouraging Decker. Sometimes, it was funny, though, and he would laugh later. This time, he only shakes his head in disgust and sips his Manhattan.

Noticing Chris's expression, Decker defends himself, "What? Don't be disappointed. I have given you no reason to expect more of me. If you do, that's entirely on you."

"From now on, I'm just going to pretend that everything you ask me is rhetorical," Chris mutters.

"Fine! You're stunting my personal growth and self-discovery, but it's fine! I can be self-actualized without you. I don't need you." Decker shakes off Chris's sarcasm.

"It's very difficult to like you," Chris responds in his best deadpan.

"Not for everyone!"

Decker grins and winks as he tips his beer to his lips. Chris's face shows his repulsion for Decker's smutty, chauvinistic response. He's referring to his recent rise in popularity with the women in the office. Chris is jealous, but not of the attention Decker's getting. Decker, despite the growing epidemic of infertility since Darkest Day, managed to have a child with his wife. It's shitty to be jealous about this, and that isn't lost on Chris, but it is difficult to avoid. Chris is also annoyed, but this is due to several things—the constant, impossible-to-ignore, pointless walk-bys and sickening flirtations happening next to his cubicle, the unneeded boost in Decker's already seemingly limitless ego, and the consistent reminder that his own life is somehow incomplete without the ability to get his wife pregnant.

Their wives' social interactions have grown increasingly infrequent. Chris can't imagine how much more difficult it must be for Cecilia to mask her emotions about other people having children, let alone her best friend. Somehow, even though Cecilia must be more affected around other people, she's better than Chris at hiding it, and he's aware of it. To Chris, his wife's strength and ability to keep her pain from making everyone else around her suffer, up until the last couple of weeks, made her even more beautiful. She is a better person than he is—this is the latest evidence, but he had always known. He is certain, though, at this point, that it's getting harder on her because, even before their last appointment, she was rarely leaving the house, and she used any excuse not to see Emily and the new baby.

Chris isn't sure that he wants a baby, even though it pains him to think it. It only makes sense to him that it would affect her more. He does want to make her happy, and his inability to do so, or even to genuinely want to have a child, is his torture. The most consuming part of his irritation is his disappointment in himself for his selfish, self-serving anger. He wonders what kind of person he must be to think about how it affects him at all, knowing full well how awful it must be for Cecilia. He hates himself most in the place where his self-pity meets his compassion for her, as people so often do when they care about another person. He imagines that the inability to have a child, for her or for anyone else who wants one, must be one of the most traumatic situations possible in this life. It is perfectly logical, he thinks, after all, it is the very nature of our humanity, ingrained in our physical and mental being from the very moment we're born. To believe your own body is defying the thing you were always told it was created to do, he can only imagine, must be nothing short of devastating, the most harrowing of personal, biological betrayals. The thought sickens him for how Cecilia must feel, yet he can't shake his own selfish objections. It makes him also wonder what must be wrong with him. Why won't his mind allow itself to want to have a child? Where in the hell is his intrinsic instinct to pass along his clearly fucked up DNA?

Emily and Decker aren't the only painful reminders. Every news story and conversation are focused solely on the growing number of people who can't have children since the CME and Darkest Day.

"Honestly, though, I can't take it. They all stare at me like I have miracle dick!"

It was undeniable—the way a few of the women at the office reacted to Decker now that he was an accomplished baby-making machine. He was always an attractive man, and that had always made him stand out. His confidence and good looks had served him well all his life. Chris was confident that Decker had only kept his job due to his charisma because it was definitely not his work ethic. This fact was evident well before Decker and his simultaneously self-proclaimed and self-denied "miracle dick" magically impregnated Emily with a child and the better part of the female staff at O.K. Package with the hope that he'd put one in them. Now, with Decker's legendary sperm and office notoriety, he pretty much does absolutely nothing at work, which is only slightly less than he was already accustomed to doing. Chris isn't blind to his hypocrisy, though, as this is the second day in a row that the two of them have sat in these seats at the bar during work hours, and it's only Tuesday.

"Yeah, I can't imagine how difficult that must be for you." Chris's sarcasm silences Decker for a rare moment before he responds.

"Yeah, well, you might be surprised. Anyway, how's Cece? You guys coming to your dickhead brother-in-law's asshole kid's birthday party next weekend?" Decker asks.

"Jesus, man! You do realize you're talking about a six-year-old, right?"

Decker takes a drink of his beer and shrugs off Chris's scolding. "I mean, he's going to be seven!"

Chris ignores Decker's statement, and in the way older couples continue an interrupted conversation with a grim look and no mention, he begins to answer the previous questions, "Cece's pretty beat-up about the fertility doctor telling her there aren't any more options. I don't know what to say at this point. I feel like a real dick because she realizes I don't want it as badly as she does, so I'm sure everything I say sounds like bullshit to her. But honestly, I'd do just about anything to give her a kid at this point."

Chris pauses to sip his beer and continues, "The whole thing is so goddamn sad! Hell, I even feel for these fucking doctors. Every one of them looks like they've been through war, just miserable and terrified. They don't have a single answer for any of those poor fucking people filling their waiting rooms, and they know it. I'm surprised any of them still have practices at this point. Long story short, she's been a wreck. She won't miss her brother's party, though. Heaven fucking forbid I would ever actually have a moment of my free time away from that piece of shit."

"Yeah, how that fucking guy is related to Cece is beyond me," Decker shakes his head.

Chris's posture collapses in on itself, defeated by the thought of standing in Tom's yard, looking at Tom's giant white teeth, listening to Tom's bullshit stories about meeting Retsel before he was "Retsel," and counting the seconds until he would be able to leave.

Retsel T. Christian and his multibillion-dollar biotech company had basically saved the world with money, technology, and their general presence. It was his tech that put out most of the fires and cleared the atmosphere of radioactive soot, and God knows what else. He controlled the weather. He made the Sun shine again. He is the unabashedly brilliant and equally handsome savior of the world. Eat your heart out, Elon Musk. After an unprecedented Coronal Mass Ejection left the entire planet in the dark, there were devastating nuclear meltdowns and uncontrollable rioting, panic, and citywide fires. Months later, when the third of the planet's population who were left saw the sky open back up, some of the lights come back on, and they found out Retsel was responsible for it, they were perfectly happy with unanimously putting their fate in the hands of his leadership.

Retsel is responsible for nearly everything that exists. He and Beta Sciences reset the entire infrastructure of the new world—every job, every company, including O.K. Package. If a person doesn't work directly for Retsel or one of his world rebuilding subsidiaries, like the communications company where Tom is a member of middle management, they work for a company like O.K. Companies like O.K. were only able to get going again thanks to Retsel's donations, and they only remain in business thanks to some level of his continued guidance. People quickly accepted the unity of direction, and normalcy fell back into place in kind.

There was an overwhelming sense of ease that settled over society as a whole—a common unspoken understanding that this new system just worked, and it did and does. The old, irritated nerve attached to the state of global affairs gave way to hive-mind calm since Beta Sciences took over. The dynamic shifted. There is no civil unrest to speak of, and the monuments made from the scars of the devastation are the only tangible reminders of what happened. People still have their own problems, and to Chris, it seems that without an uncertain world of worries to distract him, he is being forced to face his personal issues more every day.

While worrying about trying to get Cece pregnant pales in comparison to the doom-inspiring anxiety of life before Darkest Day or the horrific immediate thereafter, it is the biggest thing to worry about now. Now that the entire world has been through numerous disasters that he, and almost anyone else, can only imagine are the worst things that could ever happen, worry has changed in general. Finding a way to make Cece feel better or just not to make her feel any worse, trying to navigate through daily life without aggravating the wound of her disappointment, allowing her to heal but not sink into self-pity, and avoiding the boredom of his job while trying not to get fired, these are the problems he now faces. Though he recognizes they aren't any more or less trivial than anyone else's, the grim happenings he had been lucky enough to avoid did make his problems feel a little petty and embarrassing. His issues feel somehow insignificant, and that gives his life a levity he could not have expected.

Work seems even less important than it did before Darkest Day. Having a baby seems less important. Hell, just about everything seems a little less important, but he didn't want to be insulting to Cece—his care for her hasn't waned. At work, everyone keeps their mind on something else as well. People just mindlessly go through the motions. Maybe they always did, Chris thinks. Even Kent changed. By no means is he relaxed, but compared to pre-Darkest Day Kent, he's a little less on edge—for Kent.

Chris is painfully aware of the change in himself, but he's

been doing his best to approximate the intensity of how he always acted outwardly. He doesn't want anyone to think that he cares any less about anything. It bothers him, his resistance to feeling better. He thinks he's awful for feeling any better at all. So many people have died, the whole world twisted around itself and flipped over, and by some miraculous feat of acrobatics, it somehow righted itself. Well, Retsel righted it. Regardless, he doesn't think he should get to feel any better than anyone else, especially Cecilia. Relief for having made it through was one thing, but this isn't relief. This is something approaching some sort of satisfaction, and he has detested himself for it every day for over two years.

While Tom did work for Retsel, Chris is entirely sure that Tom never met him, at least not to the extent that Tom talks about it. Maybe he walked by, or they shook hands, but, at this point, the story was so unbelievably corrupted by Tom's bullshit that Chris was sooner to assume that it had never happened at all. He figures Tom never meeting Retsel must be closer to the truth than the unlistenable load of cock that Tom conjures, swallows, and regurgitates, fully expecting everyone else just to eat it right back up again. Even so, Chris is fairly sure that Tom does believe what he says. Tom has clearly convinced himself of it. Every "Tom met Retsel T. Christian story" would inevitably end with the same tired joke about Cecilia marrying the wrong Christian. Christian is Chris's full first name. On several occasions during these retellings, Chris imagined his hands wrapping around Tom's neck and slowly squeezing until his obnoxious laughing stopped, and the life left his grotesque smile. That being said, for as much as he hates Tom, he does feel more like his old self when he is put in a position to have to deal with Tom directly. Whenever Tom is around, Chris is distracted. He isn't burdened by the otherwise all-consuming regret for the comfort of his new "normal." He doesn't want to deal with Tom any more than he ever has, but it is undeniably grounding to feel that familiar irritation, the same irritation he felt more often than not before Darkest Day. Chris is homesick for the persistent agitation of his old life, and Tom offers a glimpse of that.

"That whole family acts like a bunch of fucking scary, asshole cyborgs designed specifically to annoy the fuck out of the rest of the world. They're all fucking creepy." Decker exaggerates a full-body quiver to accent his statement about Tom and his creepy off-spring. "Except for Julia, of course, but God only knows what's wrong with her. I mean, after all, she's got to be some sort of fucked up to want to be married to Tom, right?"

"And yet, everyone loves them and goes to all their annoying, asshole, cyborg-family gatherings. Are you going?" Chris returns the question, already knowing how it will be answered.

"Hell, yes!" Decker responds.

"Excellent," Chris replies with an intentional lack of emotion. "I don't understand why you go to his parties in the first place. It's not like you have to. I have to go. Cece makes me. But you, you don't have to go."

"The food is awesome. Free drinks. He invited us."

"He invites everyone. That doesn't mean you have to go." Chris shakes his head, annoyed.

"Em wanted to see Cece anyway. It's been a while since she's seen her."

"Still, why not just let her go? I mean, don't get me wrong, it will be less horrible with you guys there, but—"

Decker quickly snaps his beer onto the counter and turns to Chris, interrupting him. Every hint of irony and wit falls from Decker's face while he intrusively stares directly into Chris's eyes. Chris instinctively stops mid-sentence and leans away as if to save himself from some outbreak of disease Decker might be threatening to cough out at him. Decker aggressively whispers into Chris's face, which twists in confusion.

"Look, man! I want to tell you something, but you absolutely need to promise that you'll never tell anybody about it. Not like, never tell anyone, but then you go and tell your wife. Not like you say you won't, then you say it to someone you think is so out of the picture that it doesn't matter. I mean no one, like fuckin' no one!"

To Chris, this couldn't have been any more confrontational without Decker physically grabbing both sides of his collar and reeling him in the way a comic book vigilante might.

"Jesus! I get it. Calm down! I won't tell anyone. What the fuck is it? Did you fucking get Chlamydia or something?" Chris's tone switches from startled to annoyed and disgusted.

"You need to promise! I'm not kidding, man!" Decker pleads.

"Yeah! I can tell! Did you grow a second dick? Spit it the fuck out!"

Decker nervously looks around, scanning the room for anyone who might be within earshot, and he whispers, "I didn't get Emily pregnant."

Exasperated with Decker's ridiculousness, Chris doesn't bother with lowering his voice, "The fuck are you talking about?"

"I know you guys have been having trouble. It was the same for us. We couldn't get pregnant either." Decker leans closer to Chris and whispers more quietly, "She didn't get pregnant."

"What? Are you high? I saw her! We visited you in the hospital. We've seen the fucking baby, dipshit!" Chris fails to lower his voice again.

Decker whispers more forcefully as he nervously glances around, "Why don't you just tell the whole fucking bar, man? We had a baby, yeah, but not like you think. Like, the baby is ours, but we went through a company that helps people. Not a fertility doctor, but, like, they take your DNA and shit, and they make you a baby! They tell you how it all works, but I didn't know what the fuck they were talking about. I just smiled and nodded."

Their conversation pauses at the scraping of a bar stool against the tile floor. The stool smacks against the floor loudly enough to startle every patron to immediate silence and stillness. It's as if time stops in the bar for a moment before a thunderous, angry voice shouts through the dead quiet.

"WHAT ABOUT FUCKING *YIELD,* YOU FUCKING IDI-OT? WHAT THE FUCK ABOUT *NO CODE* OR FUCKING *LIGHTNING BOLT*? YOU'RE A FUCKING ASSHOLE!"

Down the bar from Chris and Decker, a large, shouting man cocks his fist back. He pushes his mammoth paw through the soft, distorting face of the man standing in front of him. The sound of the large man's fist hitting the other man's cheek is a muddy, muffled thump. The other man's body stiffens and tips as he and his crushed face begin a slow-motion journey to the floor next to the now broken stool.

A girl shouts and rushes to the unconscious body on the floor. "What the fuck, you idiot? That's my fucking brother!"

The large man lights a cigarette and throws his arms up as if to claim no fault in the situation while he marches to the door past the no-smoking sign.

"HE HAD THAT COMING FOR SO LONG! FUCK IT! I'M OUT!" Without looking back, he drops his arms to smack through the door. "WORTH IT!" he shouts with the door swinging closed behind him.

The girl tends to her unconscious brother. Heads turn back to their tables and each other. Private murmuring conversations, clink-ing glasses, and forks tapping against china quickly erupt to resume their pre-interrupted volumes.

Chris looks back to Decker, "What about her belly? Was that all bullshit?"

"Well, they gave her a fake one and some medicine to make her feel like you do when you're pregnant. She wanted the whole experience. She didn't want anyone to know, and they make you sign all this stuff that says you won't tell anyone. Other than that, they were totally cool. They help you throughout the entire process. Nothing was fake except the belly. Maya was brought to us in the hospital. I'm shooting blanks like everyone else, man!"

Chris turns back to his drink and talks to himself in paralyzing disbelief, "Are you fucking kidding me?"

Decker continues, "This place, they don't really advertise or anything. It's called Building Blocks Labs. We only found out because Em's O.B. is one of the doctors for the medical trial or some bullshit. Look, Em made me swear I wouldn't tell you, but the more you talk about it, the more fucked up I feel for not telling you. I'm sorry, man. I wanted to tell you the whole time."

"Well, great! Now that you told me, what the fuck do you expect me to do with it if I can't tell Cece? How the fuck am I supposed to do anything about it at all if I can't say you told me?" Chris struggles once again to keep his voice lowered.

"I was thinking about that. You can say you found out about it somewhere else. You can let Cece think Em had a baby the way she already thinks she did. I figure a lot of people know you guys have been trying for a long time, and there have to be more people than just me and Em who know about this thing. Maybe you tell Cece and the people at the clinic that you got an anonymous call from someone who wanted to help you, just not from my fucking phone number. I'll tell Em that you told me in confidence and that Cece's sister-in-law found out about it at the hospital. Doesn't she work there?"

"Not since they had their last kid, and Tom got his raise directly from Retsel." Chris air quotes the words *"directly from Retsel"* as he says them.

"Well then, she found out from a friend who still does. It makes no difference. Emily will act like she believes Cece is pregnant because it's supposed to be a secret between you and me, and it's not like she'll say she knows about the medical trial, or Cece might think that Em did it too. Aside from that, Cece would never even think to ask Emily, even if she did think Em lied about the whole pregnancy. That's just not something Cece would ever do, especially after going through what she's gone through. Honestly, say whatever the hell you want. Just don't say I told you about it. My dick might not be fully functional, but it still works for what I need it for, and I'd like to keep it that way."

Chris is baffled that Decker is capable of this much careful consideration and reasoning.

"Jesus, man! You really did think about this! What if Emily says something to Cece's sister-in-law?"

Decker responds more quickly with each objection.

"It's not like she'd ask her directly. I mean, Emily isn't supposed to let on that she knows, right? She would think Cece's sister-in-law is trying to keep it a secret too. If Emily did try to get it out of her, in some strange, passive-aggressive, Emily kind of way, it wouldn't matter. Julia is just going to act like she has no idea what Em's talking about because she honestly doesn't fucking know."

"No one's going to buy this shit."

Chris's naysaying is only external. Internally, he feels the same sick hope he's seen in Cecilia's eyes so many times. His weak protests are only a vain attempt to protect the moment of peace he felt with the finality of the last fertility doctor appointment.

Decker leans back into the conversation, "Look, let them believe whatever they want. That isn't the important part. The important thing is that they aren't going to ask each other about it. They'll both just go on pretending to be happy for each other, regardless of what they think. Sure, it's a lie, but how is it any different from the truth if no one ever admits to knowing it. I lie all the fucking time, so no one believes shit I say. Everyone will believe it if it's you. Plus, it would surprise you what people are willing to believe when you tell them what they want to hear."

On his way home, Chris exhausts himself thinking about how his entire life will play out with this new information. Questions pull his thoughts in every direction. He thinks of how he will tell Cecilia and how she will react. His mind explodes, uselessly littering bits of itself across an endless landscape of increasingly specific scenarios and what-ifs—what kind of cravings might Cecilia have because of the medication, baby names, daycares, schools, who will the baby resemble more, how unbelievably happy it is going to make her? He thinks about everything, everything every parent thinks. He imagines every moment—every moment from this very moment to the moment of his own death, and he wonders what his child will think of him when he is gone. He also wonders if this will be a good enough reason to allow himself to accept the repressed, pleasant calm growing inside of him. As he walks into his house, he realizes that he doesn't recall driving home, or leaving the bar, or getting in his car, or a single, tangible second of his hour commute. His anxieties are distracted by the sobering wonder of how many traffic lights he may have run. He welcomes the calm darkness of the house and the cool glow of the television.

5. Acceptance

"Hey, hon. Sorry, I'm late."

Cecilia is sitting on the edge of the middle sofa cushion, her hair half-falling out of the bun on the top of her head. He instantaneously gathers that she hasn't left the vicinity of these three cushions for much of the day, but she did make an effort to turn on the TV, and she isn't in the bedroom, so this is progress, he thinks. Light from the television flickers through the dim, early-evening hue that coats everything in the living room. Shadows and blue highlights sharpen and fade on Cecilia's face. A crumb-littered plate, a half-empty bottle of water, and a few used tissues, all lit by the blue, glowing TV, sit on the ottoman in front of her. The volume of the TV is low but not completely muted. He can hear the comforting, faint, sitcom murmurs of familiar voices and laugh track while he kisses the top of her head through the flyaway hairs.

His body lets out a mildly intoxicated, involuntary grunt as his body dumps itself next to her on the couch. Involuntary noises, he decided, were the true sign of his advancing age. These uncontrollable moans happen when he urinates. These are noises he used to hear older men making at public urinals. He was unnerved by them in his youth. Now, he is the older man at the urinal, embarrassingly squeaking out grunts, which he can hardly believe are coming from his own throat. It took a few times of him doing it, when he was entirely alone, in the privacy of his own bathroom, before he could admit to himself that the noises were his own. *"How can an old man who groans when he pees ever take care of a child?"* his mind reels again. He leans back and forces a purposeful sighing groan of breath out of his mouth. This particular noise, he meant to make it, and that is somewhat grounding to him.

Her body moves with the worn springs of the sofa as it receives his weight. She's about to say something important. It's evident in her posture, but he somehow missed it, thanks to his racing thoughts. He corrects himself to her decidedly rigid, upright pose. His hand brushes against her back as he pushes his body up to her attention. In a useless attempt to sober himself enough to listen to what she is going to say, he clears his throat and wipes his face with his other hand.

"Everything OK?"

Looking away from him so that she can force herself to say every word she must have rehearsed in her head all day, he supposes, she begins to speak.

"I don't want you to worry about me anymore. All those years, we never had an accident. I mean, I don't think this was possible, even before everything that happened. I don't know why the hell I would think it could be possible now! I think I always knew I couldn't. I think I've been preparing myself for the fact that I couldn't since I can remember.

As hard as it's ever been, as difficult as it is to say out loud, and as horrible as I feel for even thinking it, I want you to know it is a little easier now. Now that it's not only me—now that it's difficult for everyone, it's a different kind of sadness. I mean, I still want a child, and it breaks my heart, but I don't feel as alone. I can tell this is tough on you too, but I want you to know it doesn't hurt as much now that I feel terrible for everyone else who can't.

It probably sounds stupid, but I guess caring about them and knowing how they must be hurting takes away some of the pain I used to feel only for myself and the few people I knew who were like me. Maybe I was selfish. I don't know. I guess when I think about them, that selfish pain kind of turns into compassion, and maybe that's easier to handle. Also, now that I can put a definitive end to wondering if we can, it won't be as bad, you know?"

He puts his arm around her, knowing there isn't much he can say to any of this.

She leans against him as she continues, "And I'm aware I wasn't alone and that you wanted it for me more than you've ever wanted anything for yourself for as long as I've known you, and I love you for that and for everything else you are for me."

He holds her as her head turns and tips to rest against his neck. They sink back into the couch together. He hates that he hesitates to tell her what Decker told him. Eventually, he will tell her of the possibility after he makes an appointment and checks out the viability of Building Blocks Labs for himself. Aside from that, he doesn't want to interrupt her epiphany of acceptance. This is the least distraught she's been in months. He doesn't want to fill her with hope. Hope has been stripped from her so many times. What if Decker's wrong, or what if it doesn't work? These are the unavoidable anxieties that will fill her already troubled mind. He will wait and go to Building Blocks Labs alone. She came to some sort of understanding with herself, and that is a peace she's been lacking, something he will not interrupt, at least not tonight, especially since he's drunk. Until he can be sure this is real, he'll let her have this. Tonight, he'll allow their lives to be easier. With his head still floating in booze from day drinking with Decker, he pulls her body over, rests his head on the arm of their couch, and closes his eyes. He speaks quietly into her hair.

"Do we still have to go to your nephew's birthday party?"

He can't see her face, but he knows she's smiling. She nudges him with her elbow. Her voice is lighter as she speaks through a faint laugh.

"Yes, you dick."

6. DNA Solutions

Chris looks at the numbers on the door and compares them to the ones on the Post-It Note in his hand—2346. He hesitates out of nervousness and amazement as he watches the receptionist for a moment through the glass between the large numeric decals of the address. She looks more like a pristine wax statue than a receptionist. Her make-up and posture are the surreal stuff of Cosmopolitan Magazine. Her black hair is curled into a slight pompadour and parted on the right with a perfect, porcelain-white line in the same brilliant lack of color as the rest of her complexion. Her curled hair continues after the part and wraps all the way around her head, just below her ears, and then back up to the front. The office lights reflect off the manicured wave, giving it the polished-boot sheen of a new vinyl record spinning on a turntable. Her fire-engine-red dress shirt is the same shade as her matte lipstick. Noticing him standing in front of the door, she reaches for a button on her desk. Chris steps back as the door opens.

"Welcome to Building Blocks Laboratories." She stands and welcomes him with a flawless smile, her teeth bleached slightly whiter than her complexion. "How may I help you?"

He steps into the lobby, still awestruck by her immaculate appearance. He struggles to respond. She continues to smile, unaffected by his hesitation.

"Sir, were you referred to us?"

"Ah, yeah. Someone told me I should come here. My wife and I are trying to have a child."

She presses the page button on the conference phone and leans to speak into it.

"Client tour, replacement to the front lobby, please."

The woman takes a brochure and walks out from behind the desk. Another woman, just as exquisitely put together, comes from the hallway to the right of the lobby and fills the vacated spot behind the desk. The first woman nods to the other and hands the brochure to Chris.

"Hello, I'm Maria."

She points to her silver name tag and holds her hand out to shake his.

"Chris."

He briefly takes her hand as she holds out her palm, inviting him to walk with her.

"Right this way."

She leads him down a blinding hallway. The ceiling is a luminous white glow from wall to wall. The light stretches the length of the corridor and harshly reflects off the white marble floor. Thick, glass, floor-to-ceiling windows line the hallway on both sides. On the other side of the transparent glass walls, several people, covered head to toe in sterile, white hazmat style suits, are busied with microscopes, glass beakers, and Petri dishes. The workers are not distracted by the onlookers. Black, reflective plastic covers the workers' faces.

Maria's porcelain face parts between her striking red lipstick, "This is the first step in the process. I cannot allow you to view much beyond this stage. Processes and equipment beyond this first stage are strictly guarded and proprietary. Here, we combine maternal and paternal DNA and transfer it into donor oocytes, which have been stripped of their original genetic information-containing nucleus.

It all sounds quite cold and scientific, but I assure you it is a private and personal process from start to finish." She holds her hand out to direct Chris's attention to two of the anonymous, white-suited figures with face-concealing, jet-black masks as they each carefully carry one Petri dish toward a stainless-steel door behind the glass. She continues explaining as they look on, "Every precaution is taken with the utmost care. The two lab assistants bring their specific client's oocyte into the cryo-chamber."

Another lab worker opens the silver door. Fog billows out from the opening, and the two workers carry their dishes into the cooler. The door closes behind them.

"They will stay with their respective client's materials throughout the creation process. We refer to the hybrid cloning process as 'Creation.' This is an absolute last resort, though. We assume that you have exhausted every resource available to have a natural or medically assisted conception, and that is how you ended up being referred to us?" She pauses and looks at him questioningly. "That is why you are here, correct?"

Chris, astounded by everything surrounding him, stutters, "Yeah, I mean, yes, that's why I'm here. We tried everything." His words begin to race from his mouth as he nervously attempts to keep Decker from being implicated in leaking the information. "Someone must've known how badly we were struggling, and I got an anonymous ca—"

Maria interrupts him, "No need to explain. I have to ask you according to policy. We understand. We strive to enforce confidentiality for everyone's privacy, including our own, but we understand why someone who cares for you and your family would tell you. It is a breach of contract, and we take it quite seriously. Facial recognition software on the exterior of our building told us who you were. We use that and our vast information database to immediately calculate the likelihood of who told you." She pulls a small digital device from her hip pocket, presses a few buttons, and holds it out to him. A picture of Decker's dimwitted face looking into the facility's front door appears on the screen with "98% Probability" in bold font below it.

"Listen, Decker was—"

"Again, Christian, there is no need to worry or be alarmed. Decker and Julia are direct referrals from agents of Building Blocks Laboratories. We, of course, told them they were strictly prohibited from sharing information about our services with anyone, but, in actuality, we have accounted for these types of indiscretions. It's only when it becomes repetitive or unnecessarily shared that we take any action."

"Why would you tell me this? And not Decker?"

"Our research of Decker showed a high probability of him telling someone. We research our clients, as well as their known associates, thoroughly. You were vetted well before you came here today. We try not to offer all this information to everyone immediately. We don't want you to be frightened, but the data of all of your recorded history is fed into an algorithm that gives us a highly accurate look at your personality and predispositions. From these calculations, we knew threatening Decker would result in the fewest number of unnecessary secondary referrals."

"He can be an asshole," Chris mutters under his breath.

"Excuse me?" she asks politely.

"Nothing. I'm sorry. Go on."

She smiles and continues, "Your psychological profile trends toward an individual who reacts best to honesty. It is clear to us that there will be no need to intimidate you to ensure that you will be as selective as we would hope with any future referrals. We've surmised that you have yet to share this with your wife, is that correct?"

Chris nods in agreement. "Yeah, I wanted to make sure it was legitimate. I didn't want her to get her hopes up."

"Of course, otherwise, she would be here with you. If you can keep this from your wife, we believe we can safely assume the risk of you exposing our services to an excessive amount of other people is expressly low or nonexistent. Consequently, the methodology we chose for our relationship with Decker did prove to be successful, as he's only shared this information with you. To put your mind at ease, he is in no danger of us seeking any action."

"So, what's next?"

"Well, next, the donor oocyte with the client's combined DNA is transferred into a synthetic host environment where it divides and forms for a nine-month period or until the offspring, comprised solely of the client couple's DNA, is mature enough to leave the facility."

"Sounds easy enough."

"For you and your family, yes, it is quite simple. We also provide a host of services to assist you in making the process seamless for you and believable to the outside world. Our services include elegantly detailed prosthetic devices and hormonal treatments that mirror true pregnancy, from the elation of knowing she will be bringing someone into the world to morning sickness and random cravings. The process is so convincing that even Cecilia will forget she's not actually pregnant at times."

"Wait, did you just say Cecilia?"

Maria smiles apologetically, "I beg your pardon. I hope my using her name wasn't too jarring. As I mentioned, we knew quite a bit about you before you came here today. We make it our responsibility to ensure that those we choose to help deserve the assistance and fit certain criteria. We are very thorough. If we didn't know everything about you, you would have never been allowed to enter the building. I only initially asked you questions to allow you to feel comfortable. Now that you understand the scope of our process, I assumed we could speak candidly."

"Yeah, no, that's, that's fine. I get it. It's just a little overwhelming."

Chris looks back through the glass at the hive of workers.

"Christian."

Her voice steals his attention from the lab beyond the glass, and he turns back to her. Her face is calming, genuine, and vivid in the harsh lighting. He focuses on the gripping depth of her blood-red lips as their outer corners stick together slightly before they pull apart to form her words.

"This is real. You must be asking yourself, and yes, this is real. This will give you and Cecilia a child as close to the way she's always wanted it to happen as is physically possible at this point. Your concerns are natural and understandable, but this is real. You met Maya, so you've already seen what we can offer you."

.　　.　　.

Mindlessly tying his shoes at the foot of their bed, Chris focuses on Cece delicately painting mascara on her eyelashes. She doesn't notice him staring. Her expression is stoic—a brave put-on—a concealer-perfected representation of practiced pleasantry under which exists the broken but persevering heroine of a woman who wants to but cannot bear a child.

He had decided to hold off from telling her about Building Blocks Labs until he could make sure it was a true fix for their inability to conceive. Since determining that it was a real option, there hadn't been a moment when he felt like the timing was right to bring it up. He knew the truth was that timing wasn't the issue. The real reason was that he just hadn't worked up the nerve to have the conversation.

While they get ready for Tyler's birthday party, they have separate anxieties. Chris will have to listen to Tom's stories, which, while they do offer the familiarity of what life was before Darkest Day, still make him miserable, even if it is only an instinctual reaction. Cecilia will be confronted with the discomfort of listening to the conversations of several happy, yet somehow still ungratefully complaining, children-toting couples. Chris is again embarrassed by knowing the different reasons each of them has for not wanting to go and for how he had regrettably been vocal about not wanting to go. Her grounds were a million times more legitimate, and she never had and would never let on that she was, in any way, anything less than thrilled to celebrate her nephew's seventh birthday. Chris's stomach churns when he thinks about how insensitive he is for stating his gripes. He doesn't think this moment is the right moment to tell her, but with the guilt amassing in his chest, he stares at her reflection in the bathroom vanity, and his gaze catches the well of tears building on her bottom eyelids. With a racing heart, he wonders if she'll even go for it. What if she hates the idea and is offended by how much of a departure it is from how she envisioned having a child?

She dabs the corner of her eye with a tissue and inspects herself in a lit magnifying mirror, searching for any smudges in her painstaking work. His nervous hesitance to tell her is wiped away along with her welling tears. She may simply have make-up in her eye, but he cannot convince himself of the possibility enough to free him from his empathy. If he is right, or if it's even possible that going to this party with all those kids is the cause of her anguish, he needs to tell her now.

He pushes himself off the bed, stands, and walks up behind

her. She catches his reflection in the mirror and smiles over her controlled emotions.

"Look," he forces himself to launch right into it, "I think I found a way to—"

"Get out of this birthday party?" she interrupts him. "Well, you're wrong. You're going!"

She laughs, but her laughter stops short as she sees the serious look on his face. He is silent for a moment.

"What? I'm sorry. You found a way to what?" she asks.

He hesitates and rubs his hand over his mouth and weekend stubble.

"Chris, what is it?"

"Listen, there may be a way we can still have a child. I just found out about it and looked into it, and I think it's legitimate. I didn't want to"—his thoughts begin to race out of his mouth—"tell you right away before I checked it out, but—"

She smiles and grabs his hand, "Chris."

He stops rambling.

"I love that you still want to make this happen for me, but I honestly think I'm starting to accept it or that I'm coming to some sort of terms with it. I don't want to backtrack."

Every word is careful and compassionate as she tries to gently release him from what she believes is only her burden. She is so clearly grateful and genuinely concerned for his feelings that he is mortified by how much better at this she is than he will ever be. Looking at the sincerity glowing on her face, he can only think of how they are not the same—how she is beyond him in every way—how he wishes he had it in him to be this good for her.

"I don't think I can go through the hope and the let-down

again. Please, don't be upset. I get that you're just trying to make me happy, but I just can't face another doctor. I die a little more every time. I hope you under—"

"Cece, this isn't like going to the other doctors. This is different."

"That's what we always think." Her eyes plead for the conversation to stop.

He imagined this conversation many times in the past couple of days. He never made it past this point.

"But this time, it is different. It's really something you're not expecting. It sounds fucking crazy, to be quite honest, and I may actually be losing my mind, but I checked it out, I swear." He tries to equal her look of sincerity. "It works, Cecilia. It's real, or I wouldn't even think to tell you."

Excitement and terror creep over her face.

"So, what is it? You're freaking me out a little," she nervously laughs.

"It's this place called Building Blocks Labs. They have this thing where they help people like us. They are absurdly selective, and we aren't allowed to talk to other people about it, so you can't say anything to anyone. Seriously, not even your best friends."

"Whatever! I won't say anything. Just tell me already!"

Nothing makes him more nervous than the visible building sense of hope illuminating her face.

"Okay, so anyway, they take our DNA and merge it somehow, and they fucking grow us a fucking baby. It sounds insane, I know, but it's part of BETA Sciences, so, I mean..."

His nervousness is taken over by excitement for her as she looks increasingly delighted and astonished at the prospect of a real solution.

She covers her smiling, open mouth with her hands and utters, "What? Are you for real? This is a thing now? A baby?"

"Yes, I am totally serious. I wouldn't joke with you about this. I went and saw the place. I'm telling you, it's crazy. They knew everything about us already. They somehow figured out the probability that someone would tell us about it based on the people they have helped and the likelihood of who they would tell. I honestly don't understand a fucking word of it, but we can go together, and you can check it out for yourself."

Her hands and smile drop from her face. "That's really creepy. So, wait, who told you about it?"

"Some unknown number left a voicemail with a disguised voice on my work phone last week. They told me they knew we were having trouble and that I should go to this place and check it out."

"Doesn't that seem a little strange to you?"

Doubt alters her face, and he is gutted again. He tries to redirect her.

"I mean, sure, absolutely, but a lot of people know how much we want to have a baby, and you're missing the bigger thing here."

"What bigger thing?"

"If someone told us, that means they did it. They would have to know us reasonably well to think to tell us. So, we're friends with someone who went through this. It already worked for someone we know—the lady you know from your yoga class who had her kid last year—the couple from your high school reunion. Christ, two women at O.K. Package had kids this year. It could be any of them!"

"What about Emily and Decker?"

God damn it, he thinks to himself, mother fucking Decker.

He knew he couldn't pull off this big of a lie.

"C'mon, babe, if Decker knew, do you think he could keep his mouth shut about it for this long? Emily's your best friend. She would've said something. Besides, who cares who it was, they obviously want their privacy, and we're getting what we want."

Getting her to agree on Decker being weak would be his only recourse. If she doesn't buy into it, he will have to tell her and cross his fingers that she'll keep it to herself better than Decker.

"Yeah, you're right. Decker never shuts the fuck up." She laughs, and the doubt fades.

He chases her darting eyes with his, and they connect. She looks back at him, satisfied with the explanation.

"So, what do we do?"

Chris's nausea settles with the relief that she is moving past the question of whom.

"Well, if you want to go check it out, I'll make an appointment, and we can go and see the place. Then we can decide what we want to do."

"Okay. I guess we'll go check it out," she says, visibly reining in her excitement.

Gray tears jump down her face in time with the shake of her nervous laughter.

He smiles, "Do we still have to go to—"

She laughs harder, interrupting him again and growling, "Yes! We're going to the party. I guess I'll have to redo my makeup." She wipes the tears from her face with the back of her thumbs.

Chris can't remember the last time he saw her cry because she was happy.

7. Tyler's Birthday

Walking arm in arm with Chris down the sidewalk to Tom's house, Cecilia is visibly enchanted. She glows as if she's already pregnant. Her blue-with-white-polka-dots sundress dances around her legs, and she squeezes his arm in flashes of manic excitement.

"Chris, I don't know if I have ever been this happy."

"I know! I fucking love Tom's kid's birthday parties!" Chris grins.

She smacks his arm and swings around it, stopping in front of him. "I'm serious." She hugs him. "Thank you."

"Well, I didn't do anything. No one did. Not yet, at least. I'm excited too, but let's try to act normal tonight. I don't want to give Tom a reason to talk to me any more than he already does."

They lock their arms once more and continue walking toward Tom's and Julia's. Several other couples and a few children, followed by an alone and as fidgety as usual Kent, all make their way up the paved path. Tom shouts unintelligibly and waves people through the open double doors. With Cynthia propped on her hip, Julia hugs the couples as they enter.

"Aw, look! Kent made it." Cecilia reacts the same way she does when presented with happy, life-affirming videos of puppies.

"No person is more uncomfortable than Kent is right now. I don't understand why he would even want to be here. Who the fuck invited him anyway?"

Watching from a distance, as they turn onto the path to the front of the house, they see Kent awkwardly trying to navigate through the pleasantries of Tom and Julia welcoming him. Tom attempts a fist bump, and Kent flinches, dropping the oversized, immaculately gift-wrapped present that Chris watched him struggle to lug up the house. Kent's reaction isn't entirely ridiculous. Tom is well-known for his propensity for jocular punches to the shoulder and unwanted ass slapping. Julia puts Cynthia on the porch and squats down to help him pick up the gift. Kent reapplies the giant bow while Tom stands over them, shaking his head and laughing.

"Jesus!" Chris says under his breath.

"Oh, be nice! I invited him. You know, sometimes, he calls me just to check on how I'm doing? He's a very nice person." Cecilia scolds Chris with another slap on his shoulder.

"Really? He calls you?" Chris's tone is not at all jealous. He is more baffled and embarrassed for Kent than he could ever be jealous of him.

"Yeah, after our last miscarriage, he sent me flowers and a lovely card." Stating it matter-of-factly, she attempts to redirect Chris's judgment onto himself. "No one else did anything close to that."

"Awesome, I didn't realize you guys were besties. Maybe he can come by, and you two can have a slumber party." He shrugs his shoulders, mocking her with phony enthusiasm.

Cecilia ignores his sarcasm.

Kent hugs Julia, and he slides into the house past Tom.

"Maybe we will!"

Cece pulls on Chris's arm, abruptly stopping him again.

"Shit! Wait! I forgot to tell you. Tom was over the top about some kind of big surprise he has planned for everyone. I know how mortified you were when he hired that stripper for your birthday."

Chris's face sinks with disgust at the vivid memory. "My fucking grandmother was there!"

"Yeah, I know, honey. I just wanted you to keep an eye out. If it gets weird, maybe we can escape unscathed."

"She died like a week later. I still say it was his fault."

"Chris, she was ninety-three."

"Exactly my point!"

"Hey, you fuckers! This beer ain't gonna drink itself. Let's go!" Tom shouts from the doorway, waving for them to hurry.

Cece turns and waves with a smile.

"Christ," Chris grumbles again as she tugs on his arm, dragging him up the walkway. "Hey, Tom." He begrudgingly waves.

Cecilia steps onto the porch and picks up Cynthia.

"Hey, baby girl. You're getting so big."

This scenario used to be painful for Chris to watch, but it isn't today. He wonders how difficult it must have been for her to act so happy to see the little girl up until now. No one would have ever been able to tell that Cecilia wasn't entirely ecstatic to hold Cynthia. Chris could never see any pain beyond Cecilia's smile in these situations, and she looks just as happy to see Cynthia as she ever has. He thinks it must be better for Cecilia now, but he honestly can't tell the difference. Her happiness is as genuine as every emotion she displays.

Tom reaches to tousle Chris's hair as he tries to make his way into the house. He avoids Tom's intrusive touching, only to be forcefully smacked in the ass by Tom's other hand.

"Dude!" Chris scolds Tom.

"Shut up. You like it. Everybody's in the backyard. Go get a drink and relax. It's party time, bitches!" Tom tilts his head back and shouts, "Woo!"

Julia shamefully shrugs at Chris over Cecilia's shoulder while the two women hug, and Cecilia carefully passes the child back to her mother. As Julia pulls away from Cecilia, she shrinks with mortification and lips the word, "Sorry."

.   .   .

Looking across the pool, over the dozens of splashing and wrestling preteens, Chris notices an awkwardly skinny man in his mid-thirties, at most, standing by himself. The man is unfamiliar, but he's someone Chris would have surely remembered seeing if he ever had. Chris knows he doesn't know the man, but there is something familiar about him that begs Chris's attention. His face is as pointy and boyish as any one of the children at the party, and his thin-lipped smile is goofy, turned, and crooked on his face. The stranger laughs quietly but aloud to himself as he watches the kids playing. It appears that he's living vicariously through the children's collective experience. When their riotous screeching and cackling build, so does the man's obvious amusement. Though his presence is alien, it doesn't concern Chris for some reason. The stranger's awkwardness is disarming.

The man's hair is perfectly parted and cemented to his head with pomade. His pale skin is already hinting at a sunburn. His nose is bright white with zinc oxide sunblock between the blue, reflective lenses of his neon-orange Wayfarers. On his gift shop-purchased vacation t-shirt, a sailfish jumps through a blue and orange sunset with the words "Sailfish Marina, West Palm Beach, FL" written in the bottom corner of the graphic, right above where it tucks into his slightly too hiked-up, tightly tied swim trunks. There is something perplexingly amusing about this specific, featherless baby bird-looking person being dressed in casual attire. The coconut cup with a pineapple wedge, parasol, and twisty straw in his hand makes him look that much more out of place. Chris can't help but grin while he watches the peculiar character fight off his wide pencil-line smile for a moment while he pinches his drink's ridiculous looping straw between his thumb and index finger to take a sip.

After the wet vinyl smack of a toy jousting stick colliding against a child's face, a screeching shout of merriment is followed by a belly flop splash as one of the kids is pummeled off the floating platform. Chris and the strange man across the pool both laugh. The man bends forward and then back as he giggles. As he leans back, his eyes connect with Chris, who is still staring, but now, at both the child and the odd stranger. The man abruptly stops laughing and straightens his body. He stares back at Chris and slowly reaches to flip up the reflective blue lenses of his sunglasses, revealing clear prescription lenses and his squinting, concerned eyes beneath them. Chris nods and wonders if this person has something to do with Tom's big surprise. He raises his bottle of beer to the man. The man's face is locked with no expression. He slowly raises his elaborately garnished coconut cup in response.

"Can you believe this fucking idiot? I mean, who gets a seven-year-old a semi-automatic weapon?"

Chris turns to Decker, who had walked up next to him without Chris noticing.

"What?" Chris asks, still processing what Decker said.

Decker points behind them. "He got his fucking kid a Glock! Who the fuck does that?"

"Oh really? Jesus!"

Chris looks behind Decker at a huddled crowd about twenty

feet away. The birthday boy waves the weapon around, making blasting sounds as Tom shouts, "That's my boy!" Decker and Chris flinch and duck a little as the gun swings in their direction.

"Jesus Christ! What a fucking asshole!"

"Oh, so you can call him an asshole, but I can't?" Decker scoffs.

"I meant Tom, you idiot!"

Chris points at Tom, who shouts again, "Woohoo, happy birthday, Ty-ler!"

"Oh. Gotcha." Decker laughs and points to the front of the yard past the table of presents. "Would you look at this pathetic bastard?"

Past the commotion of the child with the weapon, Chris sees Kent scared stiff and inching back away from the party. After a few feet, he turns, tosses his full cup of beer into the air, and runs for the gate to the front yard. Slipping in the grass just before the door, Kent falls as his feet fly out from under his body, and he slams to the ground. Decker chuckles and slaps his knee. They continue watching Kent as he quickly scrambles to his feet and fights with the door latch. He makes several futile attempts to push through the door with his shoulder.

Tom shouts over the audible shock and terror of the parents instinctively and reasonably grabbing and shielding their children.

"Chill out, everyone! I didn't load the damn thing! What? Do you think I'm insane?"

He takes the gun from the boy's hand, releases the empty clip, pulls the slide back, and holds up the gun and clip, revealing the empty chamber and bulletless cartridge.

"Look! Nothing to be worried about."

Chris and Decker glance back to the front of the yard. Kent is gone, and the gate is swinging closed.

Decker slowly shakes his head. "That guy is one exposed nerve ending away from being an actual clitoris."

Chris nods in agreement.

Plowing through the spooked crowd, an agitated and blushing Julia reaches for and takes the clip and gun and places it back in the half-wrapped gift box. She nervously laughs, smiles at the boy, and speaks with a charming voice of reason, loudly enough for everyone to hear her.

"Okay, boys! Let's put this in the house until Daddy can take us to a safe place to learn how to use it. We can open our other presents."

Both Tyler and Tom slouch their entire bodies in the same insolent and disappointed manner.

"Aw, c'mon, Jules. It's not even loaded."

Julia grits her teeth and speaks through her smile, which is now mildly terrifying.

"Cut the cake, Tom!" Her voice is graveled with the kind of rage a man only receives from the mother of his children or his own mother.

Tom begrudgingly pats the boy on the back and hands him a butcher's knife. The boy's eyes light up at the unnecessarily large silver blade.

"Go on. Cut the cake, Bud."

The surrounding parents loosen their collective grip on their children as they cautiously inch back toward the picnic table.

Decker laughs out loud, "This fucking guy, right? Glad he's not my brother!"

Chris turns his head to look across the pool behind them. The strange man is gone. He stares, lost in thought, at the empty space where the man had been standing.

"Chris," Decker calls him back to reality.

Chris's attention snaps back to Decker.

"Yeah, don't fucking call him my brother. You know I hate that shit."

"I didn't say he was your brother. I said I'm glad he's not my brother," Decker corrects him.

"What the fuck ever. Let's get a drink."

On their way to the bar, they walk past the horrid sight of a table teeming with cake-faced children watching Tyler as he maniacally rips open present after present. A bartender in a white tuxedo shirt turns to them.

"Same thing, guys?"

Chris and Decker nod and drop their cups on the bar top. From the other side of the yard, they watch Tom regale a small crowd. Only the tail end of the speech can be heard over the music and commotion of children, but it's apparent that Tom is performing another grand reimagining of the time he met Retsel. Foamy beer suds spill onto the grass over the side of his personalized ceramic and steel beer stein as he thoughtlessly holds the absurdly ornate, stainless top open and accents his tale with theatrical hand gestures.

"...walked right up and shook his hand and told him he'd be a goddamn fool to put anyone else in charge of this district and that I'd bust my balls day and night until cell service and internet were back up to where they were before Darkest Day, or better. Two days later, I got that promotion, and not a minute too soon, cause right after that, we found out we were having another one of these rug rats."

"He is so full of shit." Decker looks away and nods toward

Cecilia. "I haven't seen her this happy in a long time. You told her about the"—he draws a pregnant belly over his stomach with his hand—"didn't you?" Decker drunkenly leans in a bit too close to Chris and loudly whispers, "You didn't say anything about me, right?"

"Yeah, I told her. Don't worry. I didn't mention you." Chris catches Cecilia's eye from across the yard, and they both grin. "She is happy. The happiest I've seen her in forever." He turns back to Decker. "Thank you for this. Seriously, man. I think everything's about to change for us."

8. Adult Time

A faint, orange glow on the horizon is all that remains of the Sun. As the natural light fades, warm, incandescent lights illuminate the paper lanterns strung from every corner of the yard. Standing in front of the cluster of orange-glowing faces, Tom drunkenly spills the better part of the contents of his beer stein in one hand while he holds the microphone from the DJ booth in the other. With the entirely unnecessary help of the sound system, his already loud voice blares over the crowd.

"All right, all right! At this time, all you kids can head into the theater room in the house. We have some kid movies that aren't even out in the theater yet, and they're queued up in the projector. We have pillows and snacks and soda and sleeping bags for everyone. Parents, I hired and wildly overpaid several of your highly qualified teenage kids, a few girls from the daycare our kids go to, and a couple of tired grandparents to look after everyone and make sure they all behave and get to bed at a reasonable hour. Consider it my gift to all of you."

The audible collective groan of the children takes over the party. Tom turns away from the crowd, still speaking into the microphone.

"Oh, well! I guess everyone wants to wait for three more

months to see *Rocket Force Three*."

The children screech with excitement and run toward the house. Tom laughs into the microphone. The adults watch as the entire cluster of screaming kids bottlenecks at the patio door. A teenage girl waves to Tom and slides the glass door closed behind the last child. Tom turns back to the crowd as they burst into applause. He embodies smugness as he grins and takes a bow.

"And there's a whole lot more where that came from, people. But first, tell me, how are you feeling?" Tom cries out.

The newly child-liberated parents nervously look at one another to see if anyone is going to answer. The DJ scratches a record, and the monotonous bass sounds of electronic dance music begin to pump through the PA system.

Tom channels the spirit of a televangelist as his volume increases, "The kids are gone, and they can't hear you. I said, tell me how you're FEELIN'?"

Decker holds up his beer and cups his hand beside his mouth.

"FUCKING WASTED!"

Tom and the rest of the crowd respond with applause, laughter, and a few approving howls.

Chris shakes his head and gives Decker the same look of indignation he generally does, but Decker just laughs and begins to dance in circles. Most of the crowd follows suit. Chris glances over the entire crowd. Every eye is glassy, every pupil dilated. They stagger collectively as a group. He finds Cecilia's sleepy eyes inviting him to join her. She laughs and slowly moves through the mix of awkwardly dancing thirty and forty-somethings toward him. He feels his head begin to swim. The crowd pushes him, brushing against his increasingly sensitive body. Each touch of the undulating blob of human flesh washes over him like a warm wave of viscous liquid flowing over his body. A strange heat grows in his genitals. He checks his crotch to see if he's pissing his pants. Again, Tom's voice comes over the speakers. This time, his words distort with reverb and drag out in slow motion.

"I put a little something extra in all of your adult beverages. Some of the highest-grade shit available. A little THC, a touch of Ex, and a bit of classic, good ol' lysergic acid. The kindly waiters and bartenders will be coming around to grab your keys. Don't be a dick. None of you will be driving anywhere tonight. Welcome to the best night of your life."

A new wave of crippling panic and dread washes over Chris, but it immediately evaporates as Cecilia grabs his cheeks and kisses him. She lets his face go and pulls him into the middle of the crowd. He moves with her writhing body in a feeble attempt at dancing, but he is not at all self-conscious. Unable to make out the faces of anyone around him who might be judging him, he feels a sense of freedom he has never known.

.   .   .

Concentrating on staying upright, Chris steers himself behind the DJ booth, whispers into Decker's ear, and picks up the microphone. Decker looks around as if he'll be chastised for his next actions if caught. He sneaks over to the absent DJ's laptop, types a few words, and looks back up at Chris.

"There are like ten versions. Do you want Cher or Frankie Valli or—"

"The fucking Walker Brothers, man!"

Chris's drunkenly irritated voice is slightly amplified through the sound system.

"Jesus! It was just a question," Decker mumbles to himself.

Chris shakes his head, scolding Decker for what he thinks was a most absurd question. The microphone rings out with mild, protesting feedback as Chris steps up onto the picnic table where the birthday cake had been.

Noticing Chris swaying on the tabletop, Tom cups his hands around his mouth and shouts over the crowd.

"FUCK YEAH, BROTHER!"

The pounding electronic beeps and bass abruptly stop. Tom's yard fills with the sound of a mariachi band brass section as if it were playing out the end of an epic western movie with the humble and triumphant hero riding slowly off into the sunset. The group of wildly inebriated adults is still for a moment as their diminished mental capacities adjust to the drastic change in the speed of the music. They pair off and begin to slow dance. Trumpets mellowly croon through the PA speakers. Tambourine, maracas, brushed cymbals, and a steadily thumping bass drum hold and accent a leisurely pace in perfect time with the trotting stride of a horse carrying a cowboy off toward the horizon.

Cecilia's laughter winds down as she realizes Chris is no longer standing beside her. She scans the swaying crowd for him. A smile extends itself across her face. She recognizes the song. This is their song. She turns away from the crowd to find Chris's face now intoxicated with not only joy, several bourbon and cokes, and an unforgivable amount of THC and MDMA, but it is also evident that the LSD has taken hold. He and almost every person at the party are now experiencing the full cocktail of drugs they unknowingly took, thanks to Tom and his party staff.

Chris looks into Cecilia's eyes from across the yard. His vision tunnels. Her eyes warp through the distance between them to his until he can only see the vacant black of her immense pupils as it surrounds him. A spotlight shines through the darkness onto him. He turns and finds Cecilia also standing in the light. They are now both dressed perfectly for a prom in the fifties. His black tuxedo, ruffled white shirt with cotton candy-pink trim, and matching cummerbund are the perfect complement to her pink, strapless, tea-length ball gown with a black-trimmed, ruched chiffon bodice and pleated skirt playfully pushed out with layers of tulle. He holds her hand and waist in proper ballroom form and sings directly to her while he dances her through the endless darkness. His voice is deep and solemn, and it resonates with a tone that he is entirely incapable of in reality. The opening lyrics to The Walker Brothers' version of "The Sun Ain't Gonna Shine Anymore" effortlessly escape his body.

Cecilia's hair and dress swing away from her, floating behind her. She smiles and closes her eyes. While they spin more swiftly with the crescendoing music, Chris feels her body leaning against his arm, giving into the centripetal force. As he belts out the eponymous chorus, Chris's voice is a hesitant, beautiful, pitch-perfect, baritone facsimile of Scott Walker's... in Chris's drug-induced delusion, but only in Chris's drug-induced delusion.

They dance and whirl through the black hole void, reveling in each other's arms. Chris is as close to pure happiness as he has ever felt.

"Hey, babe. Hey, Chris! Chris!"

Chris jolts to life in his bed. Panicked and confused, he pushes himself upright against the headboard.

"What? Hey! Why the fuck is my head fucking splitting?"

Cecilia strokes his cheek with the back of her cool hand.

"You fell, honey. Pretty hard too. Which was sad because regardless of how off-key you were, I think you were about to be very romantic."

"What? I don't know what you're even saying."

Chris's head pulses and aches with thumping arteries and the sensation of ice picks slowly pushing through his skull. He presses his palms into his temples to quiet the pain with pressure. The acidic gagging taste of liquor and bile crawls up his throat and into the back of his mouth. He unsuccessfully tries to swallow the rancid flavor back down into his sick stomach.

"Yeah, you stood up on the picnic table, got, like, two or three rather unintelligible lines into my favorite song, and took a header onto a speaker cabinet."

"Jesus Christ! I think I'm dying." Even his own words painfully bang around in his brain.

"You were out for a minute. I said we should go to the doctor, but you refused."

"Well, that all sounds plausible."

"It was super sweet of you to try to sing for me, though."

His eyes crack open to Cecilia, holding back a laugh with a horrific attempt at a sympathetic look. The swelling of his eyelids pushes them closed again.

"Oh, I wanted to let you sleep for a while, but I was too excited to wait, so I called the number on that business card you left on the table and made our consultation appointment at Building Blocks Labs. It's tomorrow morning, so you'll be late for work. I couldn't believe they were even open on a Sunday to make the appointment. I guess they—"

Chris interrupts, "Jesus! Wait, fucking Tom! That idiot drugged us." Chris interrupts her.

"Yeah, you weren't angry about it last night. Honestly, neither was I. It was nice to let loose for a change and celebrate, especially after the news. It was all very relieving. To be fair, it honestly was kind of awesome."

He pats her hand on the bed.

"Well, as long as you had fun, babe."

"I did. You did too."

"Clearly!" he groans as she walks away. "Your brother is a fucking sociopath and an asshole."

She leaves the room, waving her hand over her head and sarcastically parroting the tone of voice Chris used each of the countless times he said this before today. Her voice trails off down the hall outside of the bedroom. "Yeah, yeah, and we're all enablers. Breakfast is ready downstairs."

9. Brothers

"Are you kidding me? It was fucking awesome! Why would I be mad about it?"

Obviously reminiscing about some sort of debauchery from the night of the party when Tom drugged every adult in the community, Decker laughs and looks longingly with glossed-over eyes past Chris's shoulder to the other end of the bar.

Chris fires back at Decker, "Seriously? Why am I the only one who's angry about this? He fucking drugged us! Everyone acts like he did us a fucking favor. What if something happened, or what if someone overdosed on accident?"

"Or what if someone did an absolute nosedive-faceplant off a fucking picnic bench like a total asshole!" Decker's laughter eclipses the volume of everything and everyone else in the bar.

"Fuck you, man!" Anger, like a putrid odor, pushes up one side of Chris's top lip and broadens his nostrils.

"You were having a blast, man! Who cares if he laced the cupcakes? No one got hurt, at least not too badly. It was one of the best nights of my adult life."

"Really? Getting roofied by a psychopath is right up there with meeting your child for the first time or marrying your wife?"

Still thoroughly charmed by the dreamy reliving of what Chris can only imagine are glimpses of memories between blackouts, Decker misses the sarcasm of the loaded question and Chris's utter disapproval. The corners of Decker's mouth push slowly outward, and his features brighten with satisfaction. He nods and sips his beer.

"Yeah, right up there, man. Right fucking up there."

A foam head rises to the mouth of the bottle as he absent-mindedly places it directly onto the bar, missing the coaster by less than an inch. A chuckle gently makes his shoulders jump up and down. His head shakes the last of the reverie out of his mind, and he turns his attention back to Chris.

"So, what's up with Cece? Are you guys going through with it or what?"

"Yeah, we went in for our first appointment to meet our doctor or scientist or whatever she is. She's awesome, by the way. That's what I was doing this morning. That's why I was late for work. We go next week to give DNA."

"Shows how much I pay attention. I didn't realize you were late, but that's fantastic, man!" Decker slaps Chris's back as he tries to sip his beer.

Beer spills down Chris's chin and onto his tie. He shakes his head, wipes his mouth with a napkin, and scornfully stares out of the corner of his eye at Decker.

"Yeah, It's great." Chris's voice searches for the confidence he heard in Decker's and Cece's voices when they made similar statements.

"Jeez, man! You don't sound very excited about it." Decker hands Chris a few more napkins and points to his tie.

Looking down, Chris sees the stain. He acknowledges the hopelessness of the ruined silk and waves off the useless napkins. It's too late to salvage the tie. Worrying about it or attempting to save it is a waste of time. His shoulders collapse in on him.

"No, really, it's fine. Cece's happy, and I'll get there. I mean, I'm happy too. It's just that she hasn't stopped talking about it since we left the consultation, and I don't know, man. Am I too old to start being a dad? I'm not even comfortable getting a new car cause I'm too used to the piece of shit I have. I'm not good with change, man. What if I'm a shitty dad?"

"I mean, sure, that's a legitimate possibility." Decker shrugs his shoulders and nods in agreement.

"Well, thanks a fucking lot, man!" Chris raises his voice.

"Look, I don't know what the fuck I'm doing, but Maya is totally fine. You're not going to have to make a ton of decisions anyway. Trust me, Cece will tell you exactly what to do and exactly when to do it. You just make sure the kid doesn't touch anything sharp or put anything weird in its mouth, and you're all set. Parenting is easy, bro."

"You really are an idiot. You know that, right?"

"Whatever. All I know is Em tells me to do stuff, I do it, everyone is happy, and I look like a good parent."

"You're a real giver, Deck."

"I know." Decker puts his bottle of beer to his smug, grinning lips and finishes the last of it. Smacking the bottle onto the bar next to the coaster again, he lets out a deep belch. "Hell, if fucking Tom can keep five kids alive for this long, you'll be fine." He laughs, "I mean, it's not like you're going to give your kid a gun."

"I still can't believe that fucking guy. I've been getting up earlier for work, so I don't have to see him, and so I can make it from my house to my car without having to fight the urge to punch him in his stupid fucking teeth. I just can't deal with him." Chris angrily clutches his beer.

Regardless of how much Tom plays the role of a balancing force in Chris's daily life, Chris is actually angry that Tom drugged him. Chris is avoiding Tom, but not only because he's mad at him. Parts of Chris's brain are aware that he's holding on to his anger as a means to keep the irritating sense of normalcy that Tom's presence gives him without having to be physically near Tom. Tom would probably never apologize. He would, however, give Chris some passive, juvenile indication that he was sorry by way of a moronic and, most likely, inappropriate joke or something of that nature. Initially, Chris would be more infuriated by this, but, inevitably, it would remind him that Tom lacks the evolutionary development necessary to express any type of emotional intelligence. Then Chris would feel like a jerk, and his anger would give way to pity. He would be forced, once again, to have to see Tom to bring back this feeling. This is the way Chris's mind is wired. He knows it, and he hates it.

"Calm down, bruiser. Why don't you just give me that?" He grabs the neck of Chris's bottle and playfully wiggles it from Chris's death grip. "Let's get you a cocktail. You get all aggro when you drink beer. Let's have a nice drink and try to relax. Clearly, you're a little stressed. Plus, we should be celebrating." Decker waves down the bartender.

"Listen, don't say anything to anyone yet. Cecilia wants to wait at least a month, and, of course, we'll have to tell Tom and Julia first."

"Another round, guys?" The bartender leans toward them.

"Like I would say anything to anyone?" Decker turns toward the bartender as Chris rolls his eyes. "A couple Manhattans for me and my irritable friend here." Every word Decker utters sounds like a come-on to the attractive bartender. Chris can only assume it actually is.

"Hey, maybe we can give Tom a call. I'm sure there's something he could toss in our bourbon to put you in a better mood." Laughter pauses Decker's thought, "Ha! I bet you'll be seeing a lot more of Tom now that he's going to be your kid's uncle!"

"Oh, Christ! Fuck you, man."

After Chris's muttered response, he sighs, partly because he realizes Decker's right, but more so as a reaction to the reminder of his self-deprecating addiction to Tom's presence.

.   .   .

This is the worst-case scenario, and it's one of the several reasons Chris would have preferred to wait until he was no longer too intoxicated to drive home instead of taking a cab. There he is, Tom, in a housecoat and sandals, caught like a bold and shameless raccoon in the cab's headlights. He's holding Chris's trash can open, preparing to toss his own garbage into it.

"Not this fucking guy." Under his breath, Chris pleads with any possible deity that may exist for Tom to disappear.

Tom squints through the beams of light.

One wheel at a time, the cab awkwardly slams into the incline of the driveway. Dogs bark from neighboring yards as the tires grate against the pavement. Chris fights the door from swinging closed into his body. He struggles to catch his footing. A belly-full of bourbon and the weight of the cab door work in tandem against his will. Gripping the door, he bends himself around it and lets it slam shut. He shades his face from the headlights. The cab backs out of the driveway and scrapes its frame against the road.

Tom tosses a second bag into the can. Chris can hear the clinking of perfectly recyclable beer bottles colliding and settling into his trash. Next to the garbage can, well within reach of it, sits a bright blue recycling can. His anger builds, thinking of the countless times he's been fined for not separating the recyclables even though he and Cece are careful to never toss them in with the garbage. His fist clenches, strangling the strap of his bag. He fights the drunken urge to scream at Tom's stupid, grinning face. Pretending not to notice Tom walking toward him to initiate a conversation, Chris swallows his will to shout as he turns and walks toward his door. Behind him, he hears the snap of Tom's torch cigar lighter.

"How's the penis, bro?" Tom shouts and laughs.

Chris plants one foot onto the first step leading to his porch, but he can't bring his other foot up to the second step. He is still for a moment while Tom continues to yell from the bottom of the driveway.

"I should have tossed some Viagra in our drinks, too, huh? Then we would've had some real laughs, am I right?"

Chris turns to see Tom puffing on a cigar. He blows out a dense cloud of blue smoke. Tobacco and marijuana flavor the still evening air. Sobering rage swells in Chris's chest. His eyes focus on Tom's two giant front teeth, each one laughing with its own cartoon mouth.

Tom places the cigar between his teeth and bites down. He struggles to articulate his words around the thick, glowing stogie and the impossible, putt-putt clown teeth obstacle that is his dental situation. "Er, am I right?"

Tom bursts into laughter. Chris lets his shoulder bag and keys fall to the ground next to his foot. He pulls his other foot from the step and turns to face Tom. Purpose and adrenaline waken in Chris's eyes as he walks directly toward Tom, focused on his infuriating smile. Chris feels his heart thud against his sternum, driving an electric charge through his arteries. At this moment, he is more alive and out of control than ever. His body is reacting. His mind is a passenger riding on instinct. Without a word and perfectly in stride, all his weight and momentum merge into his arm, hurtling his fist straight at Tom's mouth. Tom is frozen in shock at Chris's fist, wheeling through the air toward him. Time slows in Chris's narrowed eyes. Tom's cartoon teeth drop his cigar to the ground, and their riotous laughter stops. They scream in terror through their fingers, cowering behind their black stick figure hands in a useless attempt at dodging the violent onslaught of Chris's fist's imminent impact. At the peak of its force and velocity, the first punch of Chris's adult life connects with Tom's face and its hopelessly terrified dental abominations. Chris's knuckles mash through Tom's jaw-dropped mouth, knocking him completely off his feet. The satisfying thick connection of the solid blow rushes up Chris's arm, and the sensation disperses throughout his body, momentarily extinguishing any trace of anxiety and tension that ever existed inside him.

Tom's big, limp body thumps onto the lawn. His bloodied front teeth click on the cement as they skid and flip down the oil-spotted driveway. Boozy intoxication floods back into Chris's head. He stares, awed at the hallucination of the animated teeth tumbling down the slanted concrete, holding hands as tears fly from the corners of their clenched cartoon eyes. Looking back up, Chris sees that Tom's housecoat came untied. A thin pair of white boxers and two-thirds of Tom's shockingly monstrous manhood are now in plain view. Equally disgusted and amazed, he manages to divert his attention from Tom's crotch, and they lock eyes. Blood paints the back of Tom's hand as he wipes his mouth and makes no attempt to cover himself.

"Oh, Christ!" Chris's guts free-fall inside of him to the edge of his asshole. The release of his tension recoils at the sight of the blood. He immediately regrets hitting Tom, and he might actually be shitting himself.

"My God, Tom. I'm so fucking sorry. I... I had way too much to drink, and I..." His voice trails off as Tom's shock turns into a quiet laugh and increases into a hearty chuckle.

"Holy thit, man! Good for you! Who knew you had that in ya?" Tom's words lisp through the bloody gap of missing teeth and his laughter. "Gueth you're thill mad about the drugging thing, huh?"

"Tom, I'm so sorry. I'm a fucking asshole. Your teeth! Shit, I'm... I'm sorry."

He apologizes again and offers his hand to help Tom to his feet. Desperately trying to avoid the spectacle of Tom's exposed genitals, Chris pulls him to his feet and onto the driveway. Tom casually pulls his robe together in front of his exposed stomach and ties the belt. With his head turned, he spits out a mouthful of blood and saliva. There is an audible splat as it hits the driveway.

"Ah! No big deal. Gueth I had it coming."

While Tom downplays the dramatic scene, Chris half-jogs to pick the burning cigar up off the lawn. He hustles back to Tom and winces at Tom's bulging lip as he hands the cigar to him.

"We should take you to an emergency dentist or something."

"Nah, fuck it." Tom waves his hand. "They aren't even real." The rubber bottom of his casual sport sandals flaps against the bottom of his feet, clacking with each step as he walks down to the bottom of the driveway, where he kneels to pick up the giant porcelain veneers. "I buthted 'em out in high thchool doing a keg thtand." He stands, and his sandals slap back up the driveway to Chris. "They're just crownth, thee?" Tom holds the teeth out, presenting them in his palm to Chris. Chris watches the teeth roll around in Tom's hand while they laugh drunkenly with x-ed out eyes and missing teeth of their own. "They'll juth glue 'em right back in." Tom drops the tiny broken monsters into the pocket of his robe.

"Still, man, I'm really sorry."

"Don't be." Tom chuckles again. "I really didn't exthpect you to be able to hit half that hard. Itth acthually kinda great to thee you act all manly. Christh, I thought you were a thyborg or thumpthin. I don't think I've ever even theen you exthited, exthept at the party when you were all drugged up. I can't even be mad at ya." He holds out his hands, one covered in his blood, a cigar in the other, and he waves Chris in for a hug.

Chris reluctantly leans into the hug, and Tom's long arms drag him the rest of the way. He slaps Chris's back and squeezes him hard enough to pull some of his weight off the ground. Blood smears on Chris's forehead from Tom's chin resting against it.

"Chrith! I love you, you crathy fucker! Brotherth, right?"

Despite his estimation of how awkward it should be to have his face nestled into Tom's neck, feeling Tom's coarse chest hair grazing his cheek and lips, choking on cigar smoke, and even with Tom's colossal cock bulge violating his belly button, Chris finds a mystifying moment of absolute peace. He is, somehow, entirely absolved of his guilt.

"Sure, Tom. Brothers." Chris squeaks breathy yelps between Tom's strong embrace and hard smacks on his back. With his arms pinned to his sides, Chris tries to return the manly back slaps, but he ends up only half-tapping, half-rubbing Tom's muscular underarm area.

Tom lets go. Air is allowed to fully return to Chris's lungs as his weight returns to his feet. The remaining teeth on the left side of Tom's mouth bite down on his cigar to hold it into place. In unison, Tom's hands smack harshly against and clutch onto Chris's shoulders.

"Goddamn right!" He smiles and exclaims out of the cigarless side of his busted mouth. His hands let go and gently pat Chris's shoulders once more. The volume of his voice lowers to suit the decreased strength of the second pat. "Goddamn right."

Tom's feet flip and flop away into his yard, up his walkway, and into his house.

．　　　．　　　．

Before Chris steps into the kitchen, Cecilia, without saying hello, launches into a series of questions that will most likely not require an answer. Her face glows behind her laptop.

"What color were you thinking for the nursery? Since we decided we're having a girl, I want it to be girly, but, like, not pink, you know? I'm building a registry for when we have the baby shower. What do you think about, like, a muted purple? I think that's what I like. Yeah, that's what I'm going with."

"Good talk," Chris responds, grinning.

He walks by her, kissing her on the cheek. Her face instinctively turns up to meet his mouth, but her eyes remain focused on the screen. Glass bottles clink in the fridge door as he opens it. They clink again as he pushes a couple of beer bottles aside to reach a bottle of water. The door closes, and he immediately opens the freezer. Ice rattles against the side of the bin. He pulls a handful out and wraps it into a kitchen towel. Cecilia looks up from the computer at Chris, wincing while he attempts to open his water.

"Water! That's a first! Ooh, what happened to your hand? Is that blood on your forehead?"

The cap on the bottle of water snaps and gives way to Chris's pained struggling. He wipes his forehead with his arm, sips the water, and inspects the clumpy blood now stuck in his arm hair. Cecilia gets up from the table and cradles his bruised and swelling hand in hers. She takes the cold compress from him and places it on the back of his hand. The towel of ice sags around his knuckles. Her face twists with compassion at his flinching hand.

"What did you do?"

"I may have punched your brother."

"Oh, that's nice, Christian! Why? Is he okay?" Her voice is more pitying than upset.

"Why? I mean, take your pick, but mostly, I had way too much to drink. Also, he's a tremendous asshole. Honestly, I'm astonished he doesn't get punched more often." Chris sips his water again, noticing that the kitchen walls are slightly tilted and spinning.

"Well, I guess none of that is particularly debatable, but he must not be that big of an asshole if you only hurt your hand. Clearly, he didn't fight back, or you'd be in much worse shape."

"What's that supposed to mean? I can defend myself!"

"Chris, honey, I love you, and you're all the man I'll ever need, but he's like a monster. He'd kill you. Did he even try to hit you back?" She frowns patronizingly at him while she waits for the answer.

His face tilts downward, stripped of the offense it took a moment ago.

"No. He laughed. He laughed"—his face raises back up to meet hers—"and then he hugged me." His tone cools to equal parts matter-of-fact and sheer embarrassment as he realizes how weak this statement makes him sound.

"Awe!" She smiles and cocks her head to the side, obviously trying not to laugh in his face.

"Hey, it was a real punch! There was bleeding, okay? I don't need your pity. It did knock out his two front crowns, all right?"

"I don't know if I can truly express how proud of you I am right now." Her face is painted with a thin, false candy coating of sincerity that struggles to mask her body-shaking laughter.

"Hilarious," he scoffs.

Cecilia reaches behind him, halfheartedly rubbing his back. "Oh, I'm sure it really did hurt him, honey."

"I hope our child gets your sense of humor," Chris deadpans.

She stands up from the table, gives him a few soft, reassuring pats on his shoulder, and leaves the room.

10. A Unique Conception

"Mr. Adams, please have a seat in one of our private waiting rooms."

The nurse holds her arm out to a series of identical glass doors lining the right side of the hallway. She motions for Christian to step into the first waiting room. Cecilia stops and looks back at Chris as he opens the door. Her nervous stare stops him. The nurse places her hand on Cecilia's back.

"No need to worry, Mrs. Adams. You already did the cheek swab. That was as close as you will have to anything resembling a medical procedure from this point forward. I hope this was clearly explained to you during your first consultation appointment last week?" Her expression is warm and comforting.

"Oh, yes. Everything was explained to us perfectly. Doctor Magus was lovely and extremely thorough. Sorry, I'm a little nervous." Cecilia laughs and raises her eyebrows, "I guess I'm just feeling a little exposed." She reaches behind herself and pulls the white hospital gown closed to hide her underwear and backside.

"You'll be fine, hon, and you've never looked better," Chris grins.

Cecilia shoots him a humorously annoyed glance. "Thanks!"

"I assure you there is no reason to be nervous. All we will be doing is mapping the features of your body to fit you for your prosthetic bellies. You'll be wearing them for nine months. We want to be sure the fit is perfect so that you'll be comfortable, or rather, as appropriately uncomfortable as you should be during each stage of your pregnancy. In simple terms, we will only be taking a few pictures. Still, Doctor Magus will be present during the entire procedure."

"See, honey, just a few nude pictures. Nothing you haven't done a million times," Chris adds with a giddy smirk.

She shoots him the same look of amused irritation as before. "Don't get your hopes up, pal. You're never going to see them."

The nurse maintains a pleasant, professional smile and guides Cecilia down the hall. Chris watches them for a moment, listening to the nurse trying to ease Cecilia's mind while the two walk away.

"The images will only exist in a digital form, and once everything is fabricated, the information is erased. No person, including myself, will see these images."

Chris steps into the waiting room. As the door closes, the glass becomes hazy and white. The view into the hall is completely blurred.

·   ·   ·

Cecilia glows as she enters the waiting room. Christian closes the magazine in his lap and tosses it onto the table with the others. He stands and imagines her moving in slow motion, her fine curly black hair slowly bouncing against her pale cheek. She tucks the curl behind her ear and looks at him. Her red matte smile separates and extends, exposing her bright teeth and forcing her cheeks upward to squint her eyes with merriment. Immediately, Chris is, once more, made fully aware that this is as happy as she has ever been, even before Darkest Day.

Doctor Magus follows Cecilia into the room. The nurse closes the door behind them. The doctor's presence is sterile. Her face is perfectly sculpted and shadowed without a hint of make-up. Chris is at ease around her. The confidence in her intense blue eyes, paired with her detailed explanations of everything, leaves no room for doubt or error. She's cool and collected in a way that makes Chris wish everyone was. Life, in general, would be so much simpler if more people were able to be this clear, concise, and level-headed, he thinks. He's slightly jealous of her lack of emotion. He wishes he, too, could be more like her.

"You're all set. Go home and start getting ready to have a baby. Cecilia, everything you'll need until next month is in the bag the nurse provided you." She gestures to the tote bag hanging from Cecilia's shoulder. "Take the medication once a day, as directed. They will allow your body to produce hormone levels, which will basically mirror that of any pregnancy. You'll even experience moderate weight gain and intense cravings for different foods. In public, please follow the diet restrictions so that you won't raise any eyebrows. I will see you each month, but we will meet at a different office. The address is provided on the paperwork in your tote. There, you will also find other helpful materials to read at your leisure. We threw a few goodies in there too. A word to the wise, dad, moms love gifts. And be sure to check out the coupons. We know how much this costs you, so we do what we can to provide you with some generous discounts on many of the items you'll need. We will gauge your progress and weight gain next month and begin the use of the prosthetic. Do either of you have any questions?"

Cecilia looks at Chris, who gives her a muted shrug.

"I don't think I have any right now," she answers.

"You will, and when you do, don't hesitate to call the office. We'll see you next month. Congratulations!"

"Thank you," the couple responds in unison. They take turns

shaking the doctor's hand.

She directs them to a door on the other side of the waiting room. "Please leave through the private exit here, and your vehicle will be there waiting for you."

She holds the door for the couple. Cecilia and Christian smile and wave to her as they get into the Corolla.

"My God, Chris! We're going to have a baby!" She smiles with tears threatening to spill from her eyes, and she embraces him over the center console armrest.

Dull panic tightens his chest, but he smiles back at her. This is the new reality of their lives. There is going to be a baby. He no longer needs to seek distractions from his peace of mind. He is distracted. Until now, he only had to be sympathetic about the fact that they couldn't conceive. Now that all the fears and anxiety he conjured up the night he found out that they might be able to have a child are no longer hypothetical but terrifyingly real, his mind teeters between excitement for her and dread for himself. In their years of trying, he could never imagine being a parent. Many parts of him preferred it that way. After coming to terms with the fact that he was no longer going to have to consider the possibility of becoming a father, he is, once again, forced to torment himself with the punishing self-doubt of whether or not he is even capable of being one. She won't be allowed to see his doubt. He decided this to himself as soon as Decker told him. Regardless of how scared he is, he will not let it ruin this for Cecilia. She's been through too much, and honestly, how hard could it be? Decker was managing it. There was no way he could be worse at being a dad than Decker. As he turns the car onto the street, he laughs out loud at the thought of Decker actually having to parent a child.

"What are you laughing about?"

"Nothing. We're having a baby!" He tries to match her excitement and does it convincingly, "I'm just happy for"—he thinks to say, *you*, but manages to substitute it with—"us"—in perfect continuity. His correction is imperceptible.

She laughs, "I know, right! Me too."

She reaches over and squeezes his hand on his lap.

"Last night, I started putting together a list of everything we're going to need. I mean, I'm sure Julia will have a ton of hand-me-downs, but I'd prefer some things to be new, you know? Oh, and this car is not going to work. We need something safer. Do you think we need a bigger place? I guess we could turn the office into a nursery…"

These are rhetorical questions, and this is made clear by the lack of pause for an answer and the frantic speed at which they are posed. He strains to focus, attempting to understand and catalog each concern for a future response, but he loses his ability to recognize what she's saying. Her words run together with his compounding thoughts, and it all merges into a single, incomprehensible, white noise ringing. Even looking directly at her mouth, it's impossible for him to discern any particular words over the persistent tinnitus piercing his eardrums. He nods, smiles, and does his best to direct his attention to the road in front of them.

11. The Announcement

Intermittent scrapes and clinks of metal against plates become more infrequent. The two couples sit across from each other at a dark mahogany table under a simple, elegant, crystal chandelier. From directly across the table, Chris studies Tom's face while Cecilia and Julia pick at their mostly empty plates. Tom's chair creaks under his shifting weight as he leans back. He rubs his belly, sighs, and moans along with the straining wooden joints. His plate is as clean as it was before they sat down to eat. Chris had silently suffered through the entire meal. It was impossible not to watch on in horror at the grotesque spectacle of Tom eating. He breathed intensely through his nose while stuffing his mouth with mangled piece of bread after mangled piece of bread that he used to sop up every drop of liquid left on his plate from his steak, corn, and the smears of mashed potatoes and gravy. He left nothing behind except the shiny white, gold-trimmed porcelain of his plate and the echo of sloppy mouth noises in Chris's mind.

"Okay, guys, time for an announcement. I... we"—Cecilia corrects herself, glancing at Chris—"wanted you guys to be the first to know."

There is no visible evidence of Chris's punch on Tom's face. On Tom's side of the table, it's as if nothing happened. On Chris's side of the table, he is still finding it difficult to hold his knife firmly enough to cut his meat. He glances down at his bruised fist and then back up at Tom's mouth, annoyed at its lack of any proof whatsoever that it had been hit with all of Chris's strength. His two front teeth look slightly larger, but Chris wonders if it's just his imagination. The vile, wet screech of Tom tonguing and sucking at the bits of food stuck between his newly crowned front teeth is unbearable to Chris. As he focuses on it, the sound amplifies in his mind until Tom's mouth noises are the only audible thing to Chris. His face wrenches further into the pits of disgust. Cecilia tugs at his arm. She scolds him with a quick, sour look. Realizing that he is staring at Tom with bold disdain, he corrects his face with a pleasant smile and sips his wine. Julia already dropped her fork onto her plate and put her hands over her mouth to hold back her excitement. It's apparent that she knows what is about to be said, but she restrains herself until Cecilia is able to finish the announcement.

"We"—she looks over to Chris again and back to Julia— "We're having a baby!" By the end of her sentence, she is shouting with Julia, whose hands dropped away from her face with the first hint of the first B in the word baby being formed by Cecilia's lips. They both stand and scream at a shocking volume and pitch while they half-run, half-dance around the table into each other's arms.

"Oh! I just knew it! I said to Tom, watch, Cecilia's pregnant, and he said, 'No way!' but I told him. A mother can tell. A mother can always tell. Didn't I, Tom?"

"Sure did, Honey!"

Tom and Chris stand and join the hugging women at the end of the table.

"I knew it. I'm so happy for you." Julia releases Cecilia and latches onto Chris. "For both of you."

Tom hugs Cecilia, "Welcome to parenthood, sis. It's all downhill from here." He lets her go and steps toward Chris. "You aren't going to try to hit me again, are ya, Holyfield?" After imitating a boxer ducking a couple of jabs, he grabs Chris's shoulders and gives him a solid shake. "You finally did it, you baby-making son of a bitch!" He pulls Chris into his clutches and crushes him with a bear hug. A stern blankness erases his expression as he pushes Chris away and continues to hold him at arm's length. "I'll only give ya one word of advice."

"Sure, Tom."

Tom leans in with his face, still completely void of any expression. "Keep your head up, brother." He shakes his head up and down as if imparting some remarkable wisdom.

"You mean like, stay positive? That kind of thing? Sure," Chris feigns to understand but isn't quite sure what Tom means.

"No. I mean, like, literally. Keep your eyes up. Don't go in there with the idea that you might wanna witness the details of this shit going down. You clear that thought right out of your head, quick. I peeked down there with my first one, and God damn." Tom's head shakes back and forth, his face covered in apocalyptic foreboding. "Trust me. You couldn't handle it."

Julia playfully slaps Tom on the shoulder. "Don't try to scare him. It's not that bad. Ignore him. It will be the best day of your lives."

Tom's face snaps back into excitement. "This calls for the good stuff. The kids are all gone until tomorrow, and I got a couple of Cubans and a bottle of Louis that Cecilia can watch the rest of us enjoy. You two finish up and meet us out on the deck."

Without much of a struggle, Chris unenthusiastically tolerates Tom reaching around his neck, putting him in a half-nelson, and dragging him into the next room. Chris forces a smile, pushing back his irritation and knowing he is only being tortured as a side effect of Tom's merriment, or, more accurately, Tom's oblivious merriment paired with his incapability of respecting even the slightest amounts of personal space and decorum. As much as Chris protests to himself, this is all quite comforting to him.

"Hell, you should be congratulating me! I am gonna be a fuckin' uncle! Woo hoo!"

With the moist heat of Tom's armpit on the back of his neck, Chris surrenders a sincere laugh for Tom's unadulterated joy.

"Congratulations, Tom." He awkwardly stumbles along Tom's side.

"Ha! Yeah! Goddamn right! Tonight, my brother from another mother, we drink like kings!" Tom snatches a shapely bottle from a red pedestal on the top shelf of the bookcase in the den.

Crystal ribs outline the upside-down heart-shaped bottle filled with blood-colored alcohol. It's embellished with several fleurs-de-lis and topped with a crystal stopper with the same design. Tom bought it for a little over two thousand dollars after impressively, in Tom's own words, talking the guy down from over four thousand. He purchased it to celebrate his last promotion and swore not to drink it until his next one. Chris knows this because Tom explained this to everyone he's ever spoken to, including Chris, on multiple occasions. The details varied drastically with each retelling, not unlike the rest of the story of his promotion and the time he met Retsel. Apparently, becoming an uncle serves as a momentous enough occasion to merit opening his prized Louis XIII Cognac. Tonight, they will, quite literally, drink like kings.

12. Eight-Month Check-up

The Allen wrench clinks against the wall. Chris's fist slips, and the corner of the crib frame gouges into his knuckle.

"Son of a—"

"Watch it." From the doorway of the light purple nursery, Cecilia interrupts Chris. You're going to be a daddy. You can't be cursing all the time like before."

"I won't have to worry about that if I kill myself putting this stupid fu"—he stops himself—"this crib together. I swear I'm being tested to see how much bull"—he stops himself once more— "irritation one person can take. I'm never putting another piece of furniture together as long as I live."

The crib's headboard stands at a forty-five-degree angle, propped up with the bed rails, which rest on the carpet near several other pieces of yet-to-be-assembled bed parts. Chris finds the Allen wrench on the floor, stands up, and grunts, realizing how sore his lower back is from being in the same hunched-over position for the better part of an hour.

He sees Cecilia in the doorway, radiating her pregnant glow into the room and holding a pint of ice cream with the handle of a serving spoon sticking out of the top. Though he tries, he can't imagine a satisfaction for himself that could ever make him appear as complete or purposeful as Cecilia does right now, as she has for the past eight months. Her mouthful of ice cream may be adding to her palpable joy. She also looks every bit as eight months pregnant as any woman who's ever been eight months pregnant. Her shoulder leans against the door frame to take a little of the extra weight from her fake but entirely believable belly off her feet and lower back. She tucks a few waves of her chin-length, black hair behind her ear. Her typically sharp features are pleasantly rounded from her actual, hormone-induced weight gain. The weight gain is minimal, but Chris can easily see it, and it only makes her look even happier and brighter. She smiles, sets her ice cream on the drawerless dresser, and pushes her belly out with her hands on her sides. Her body turns provocatively, and she slides her back against the door frame, revealing her bulging profile.

"Would you like me to put it together? I could, you know."

"But then who would eat all the ice cream and correct me every five seconds?" he laughs.

Mildly straining, she pushes herself away from the door frame. Snatching the ice cream from the dresser, she turns sharply away from him, pretending to be offended. She looks over her shoulder and jams another heaping scoop of chocolate with peanut butter swirl into her mouth.

"Well, it's not going to eat itself!" she mumbles while trying to keep the melting ice cream from dribbling down her chin.

Chris pulls the bed rails up off the floor, standing the headboard straight up while she walks away. He pulls the unattached footboard over to the other boards. Holding the footboard with his knees, he stretches his arm across the floor to grab a long screw that is barely within his reach.

"Hey!" Cecilia pops her head into the room, startling Chris in mid-reach.

The footboard falls onto his back, he drops the Allen wrench again, and the headboard detaches from the bed rail he's holding and slams to the floor. He looks up at her with the footboard still leaning against his crouched body.

"Yeah?"

She covers her mouth while she belly-laughs at the mess of boards and his angry expression. Between laughs, she takes her hand away from her face just long enough to say, "Don't forget we have the eight-month check-up tomorrow."

Pushing the footboard off his back with his left hand, he reaches under himself with his right and gives her a thumbs up and a big, fake grin.

She places her hand back over her mouth and continues to laugh as she walks away.

·   ·   ·

"Well, it's been eight months. You're almost there. How have you been feeling, Cecilia?"

"I feel like a broken tank. It's difficult to move and even more difficult to be still, especially when I'm trying to sleep. My feet are swollen. My back is aching. I'm hungry all the time. I have to pee every two minutes. I have to pee right now. I chew Chris out about everything. Then I cry cause I feel bad about it, then I cry cause I'm happy he still loves me even though I just chewed him out. Then I have to pee again."

For spouting such a laundry list of things that, on paper, would read as complaints, her lips are oddly frozen in a smile while she inventories each item for the doctor. She pauses to glance at Chris and turns back to Doctor Magus.

"It's been unbelievable." She squeaks and giggles with the pitch of an excited toddler. "I've loved every second of it. This is truly the absolute greatest feeling I've ever had. Thank you so much, doctor."

"No need to thank me. You did all the work. I can see that you did very well with everything I asked of you. The blood and hormone levels the nurses took today are perfect for this stage. I trust the prosthetic attachments have been as comfortable as they should be, mind you, that's not particularly comfortable?" The doctor smiles and forces an insincere laugh.

"Yes, they're incredible. It's just like you said—sometimes even I forget they aren't real, especially when she kicks!"

"Perfect. Yes, the motorized units produce every movement a baby makes at every stage of development. I hope you have been able to share some of those precious moments with your family." She looks back down to her reports and flips to the next page. "Your weight gain without the prosthetic is right in the middle of the range where we were aiming." She looks back up at them. "We are right on target in every way."

Cecilia squeezes Chris's hand with nervous excitement.

"Your supplements and hormones will vary slightly for this last month, and the new prosthetic belly will drop a little lower. You'll notice some changes, but it won't be anything you can't handle. You will also be coming in once a week for these final four weeks to keep up appearances as this is routine for a normal pregnancy. I will be on the premises during your visits, but we won't need to meet unless you are having issues or need me to answer any questions or concerns. Otherwise, the nurses will check your hormone levels, and you'll be free to leave. If there are no problems or concerns, I'll see you on the delivery day. The delivery is completely planned, and your date is set for your arrival at our hospital. Just a reminder, it is totally private. Feel free to invite friends and family, but only the two of you will be allowed in the delivery room at the time of delivery. Everyone can visit when you're moved to your recovery room. Do either of you have anything at all that you'd like to discuss today?"

Chris looks to Cecilia, who is already shaking her head no. He turns to the doctor, "No, doc, I think we're good. Hopefully, we won't be meeting with you again for four weeks."

She walks around her desk and opens the door.

"Excellent! All three of you are going to be great."

13. The Baby Shower

Clutching the arms of the lilac rocking chair, Cecilia strains to push herself, belly first, out of her seat. Chris notices her struggling and rushes over to help her. He spills his pink plastic cup of mimosa while trying to set it on the table and gets to her just in time to be of absolutely no use.

"I'm good." She laughs at his nervous overreaction.

"Sorry." With one hand on her arm and one on the small of her back, he guides her out of the nursery through the stacks of brightly wrapped gift boxes and bags with pink tissue paper sticking out of their tops.

"Can you believe all this stuff? There's no way we could ever use all these newborn clothes, but they're so freaking adorable. I can't even handle it. Did you see those little sneakers? They're so itty-bitty!" She grabs onto his hand on her arm and excitedly shakes it.

It's impossible not to get caught up in her hysteria. He laughs, "Yep, they're pretty freaking adorable."

They turn the corner into the kitchen. A few plastic cups and paper plates are scattered on the coffee and end tables. Julia crosses their path with a white garbage bag, picking up the abandoned items.

"Thanks so much for everything, Julia. You don't have to clean up. You already did so much." Cecilia places her hand on Chris's shoulder.

"Yeah, Jules. We appreciate it. The whole shower was amazing. We can pick up."

"Guys, it's not a problem. I have to clean way more than this at my house on a daily basis. Between five normal kids and one big man-baby, our place is always a disaster. This"—she holds up an empty cup and drops it into the trash bag—"is like a vacation. Plus, the dishes are already handled." She nods her head toward the kitchen and grins.

Chris and Cecilia peek into the kitchen. Kent is dancing in front of the sink as he dries the dishes he presumably washed.

Kent sings in falsetto with his butt bouncing to the beat playing in his headphones, "Get you milk-drunk off my uh. My bump, my bump, my bump, my bump, my bump, my bump, my bump, my bump. My little baby bump."

As he turns to hang a pan over the kitchen island, his frill-trimmed pink apron is revealed. Bold black letters on the chest of the apron read, "Real men wear pink."

His voice awkwardly tapers off as he notices the three faces staring at him from the next room. He shouts over the song in his headphones. "Oh, hey, guys!" His hips come to an embarrassed stop, and he pulls out his earbuds. "Just helping clean up."

"Kent, did you bring your own apron?" Chris's face is locked somewhere between confusion and disbelief.

"Yeah, I keep one in my car for emergencies. Why?"

It's clear by the tone of naivety in Kent's question that he imagines this is a common practice for all people.

"What? Why? Is that weird or something?" His innocence

gives way to his twitchy, overpowering nervousness.

Chris and Cecilia lean their heads back out of Kent's line of sight.

Kent shouts in the direction of the living room. "So, I... I'll just finish up here and take out the trash and get going. Let me know if you need anything. Maybe I'll sweep out here too."

"It's like someone crossed every wire in his head and set him loose on society," Chris states quietly enough for only Cecilia and Julia to hear him.

"You shush!" Cecilia punches Chris's arm. "He's sweet, and at least we don't have to do the dishes."

"I just want him to leave so we can take those down." Chris points to four life-size cardboard stand-ups of Chris's and Cece's parents created from awful, enlarged family portraits. Pink balloons tied to the hands of the cut-outs float on each side of both sets of deceased grandparents.

"There are no words." Julia snorts, covers her mouth, and joins Chris in shaking their heads and laughing at the strange gift from Kent.

"Oh! Not you too, Jules. I think it was so nice of him to do that. It was nice to have them here for the party. He knows how much I wish they were still around to see this," Cecilia pleads with her sister-in-law.

"I'm with Chris on this one. It's so not normal."

"Not normal? It's fucking bizarre! Babe, when he asked you for those pictures, you didn't think it was a little weird?"

Both Chris and Julia look to Cecilia, waiting for her to answer.

"Well, maybe a little, but he always has good intentions, so I just assumed he was doing something nice, which he was."

"Do you two remember how messed up we were at Tyler's party when your insane brother and husband drugged all of us?

"We all remember how fucked up you were!" Julia smacks her leg and doubles over laughing.

Cecilia bites her lips and covers her mouth to hold herself back.

"Yeah! Hilarious! Anyway, Kent had just as many drinks as we did for the first half of that party, and I definitely saw him eat one of those cupcakes they passed around to the adults."

"Yeah, so, what's your point?" Julia says through the coos of her fading laughter.

"My point is, he ran out of there before Tom took everyone's keys. The next Monday, I asked Kent how the hell he got home with a headful of acid, and do you know what he said?"

"What?" The women ask simultaneously.

"He said he didn't notice anything at all out of the ordinary. He just went home and watched the news and went to bed. That can only mean one of two things, either the same crazy cocktail of psychotropic and hallucinogenic drugs that had every single other person at that party totally tripping balls didn't affect him, or he's just so out of his mind on a normal basis that it didn't seem any different to him."

They all look back out into the kitchen. Kent is still singing in falsetto into the handle of a broom as he sweeps and dances across the tile floor.

"What you doing with all that, Huh? All that uh inside that what?"

"He's broken," Chris assures them.

14. The Delivery

"Do you have any other questions or concerns before meeting your beautiful baby girl?" Even in this intense moment, Doctor Magus is perfectly dry and even.

Cecilia clenches her hands together over her chest. Her excitement is contagious. Chris is caught up in the moment as well. He finally feels the rush of endorphin release as happiness takes over his apprehensive nervousness. Cecilia grabs his hand. She's trembling. Her palm is cool and wet, her eyes wild with excitement. She is understandably exhausted and slightly leaned back in the hospital bed. Tiny beads of sweat still shimmer across her forehead from the struggle of the chemically induced, false contractions and labor pain.

Chris wonders how much of her reaction to the baby will be artificial—created by the mix of hormone injections and sedatives they gave her to make her feel the way any laboring mother would. To him, the pained howling and moaning seemed terrifyingly genuine. After witnessing that undeniably horrendous torture, he sees little distinction between this and how real labor has always been described to him. He guesses it doesn't matter how much of this was brought on by unnatural means. It was as brutal and arduous as anything he's ever seen. As far as he is concerned, she is as real a mother as any, and she deserves every bit of joy that could stem from the misery she just endured out of only the pure, honest desire to be a mother. If there was a difference between having a child the way she did and having one any other way, it no longer matters.

Chris's awe of Cecilia forces a realization of how greatly this part of life affects every person who has ever been part of creating or caring for another life. For the first time, he understands the scope of their connection to the rest of humanity. Their existence is bridged to everyone else. They are linked to people who desperately want children and cannot have them, to people who empathize with it deeply enough, even without having been through it, that they would take care of someone else's child as their own, to people who have had the most straightforward path from wanting to having a child, to people who choose not to have children because they truly and realistically grasp the weight of such tremendous responsibility, to every living being. Tears well up in his eyes, and he knows he is forever changed.

"I think we're ready!" Cecilia shakes Chris's hand and looks over at him as she answers Doctor Magus.

"Absolutely!" he forces the tone of excited sincerity with the pressure in his chest and the growing lump in his throat.

One of the nurses opens the delivery room door and holds it with her foot. A black, frisbee-sized drone hovers into the room above and in front of another nurse in surgical scrubs. Chris doesn't recall being told about a drone at any of their appointments, but Cecilia doesn't appear to be off-put by it in the least. He assumes he must've missed it or forgotten about it. Still, the drone's presence, the glowing red light on top of it, and its whirring propellers in the intimate setting of their delivery room make him anxious. He wishes he had paid better attention. Maybe he would have been more prepared for it. By the nurse's eyes, it is evident that he is smiling behind his surgical mask. As he comes closer, Chris can see the nurse is cradling an empty, white newborn baby blanket wrapped only around itself.

Cecilia holds her hand over her mouth. Tears stream from the corners of her eyes and roll over her flushed cheeks. Her body shakes with excitement and laughter. Chris squints his eyes to inspect the rolled fabric in the nurse's arms. There is nothing in the blanket. The nurse carefully places the cloth on Cecilia's chest. The new mother's face is soaked with tears. She is perfectly enamored, looking at the empty folds of the blanket. *"What the fuck is happening?"* Chris's mind races.

Cecilia glances up. "Oh, my God! Chris, she's beautiful!"

Instinctively, he smiles back at her, but in his head, his mind is unhinging. He manipulates his features to put on an excited and shocked face. His excitement is forced, but his shock couldn't be more candid.

The knot twists in Chris's throat, blocking the sterile hospital air from entering his lungs. Careful not to draw any attention to himself, his eyes quiver and dart around the room. Desperately, he scans each of their faces for any sign that any one of them is seeing what he is seeing. There's no evidence. Every other face shines with the expected sort of joy that he imagines the revealing of a new child should evoke. Whispered shouts of *"Congratulations"* and *"Oh my God! She's so cute! Look at the baby!"* echo in his mind. Their attention is thankfully on the baby rather than on Chris's reaction to the nonexistence of a baby. If they stopped to inspect his face, they would find an expression of pure panic. He begs his mouth to curl at the ends, his eyes to narrow, his lungs to breathe, his presence to be consistent with everyone else's in the room.

He's not seeing what they must be seeing. The only thing holding him back from screaming is that Cecilia evidently sees the same thing as every nurse and doctor in the room. *"This must be a psychotic break! What are they looking at? My God, what's wrong with me?"* His mind drowns in shock, trying to organize his confusion. All color drains from his face. His body collapses. The bright room fades into darkness as he plummets to the tile. The steel railing of the bed lets out a single, reverberating church bell toll as his head caroms to the floor between the bed and the heart monitor. The blow simultaneously wakes him from fainting and knocks him nearly unconscious. He lies on his back, watching the concerned faces of Cecilia, the doctor, and the nurses looking down at him. With his reality quickly dissolving, once more, into absolute black, time seems to slow. The doctors and nurses kneel over him with their mouths moving behind their masks, and Cecilia's lips form concerned shouts, but their voices distort and pull away from him until they are faint, muted echoes. He feels his eyes slowly rolling into the back of his head and his body sinking into the floor. The last thing in his line of sight is the drone's silhouette as it eclipses the final bit of light left between the doctor's, nurse's, and Cecilia's heads. The floating machine scans a band of red laser light over his face just before he completely loses the last remaining vestige of his failing consciousness.

·   ·   ·

The dim light of the bedside lamp is blinding. His eyelids slowly peel apart. He cringes at the light and his pulsating head and clamps his eyes closed again. A moan involuntarily creeps out of the back of his throat. The throbbing pain extends to the center of his brain from a point just above his right eye. He reaches for the source of the pain and finds a small bandage at the peak of a golf-ball-size lump. Another hand smacks his hand away from his forehead.

"Dude! Don't fuck with your stitches."

Decker's voice is immediately recognizable to him. His eyes reopen, but he struggles to focus on his friend standing over him.

"What the fuck happened?" Chris's pounding brain tries to assemble his memories into something coherent.

"Man, I heard you biffed it, hard, off the bed railing. Then you smacked the back of your melon on the floor. Your eyes are like, totally black!"

Decker's wincing face comes into focus.

"I fucking told you, bro! I told him! Keep your head up. Didn't I tell you?"

Chris's head feels separated from his body. He turns it to see Tom leaning back in a chair with his feet propped on the bed and his face behind a magazine. The magazine folds away from in front of him.

"You looked, didn't you? I warned ya, bro!"

Memories of the drone and the fear from the delivery room converge, full force, into the pained lump on Chris's head. He lunges for Decker's arm and instantaneously regrets moving so quickly. Decker is startled. The throbbing in Chris's head intensifies, dizzying and nauseating him, but he pushes through the debilitating vertigo to hold himself at attention with a death grip on Decker's wrist. Pale and struck with panic, Chris's eyes plead with his friend.

"Did you see the baby?"

"Dude! Relax. Everything's fine." Decker tries to calm him.

"Decker, did you see the baby?" Chris strangles Decker's arm with a quick jerk, pulling him closer to the bed.

Decker attempts to pull away but doesn't escape Chris's grasp.

"Yeah, man. Yeah, I saw her. She's doing fine. Calm down!"

Someone touches Chris's shoulder from behind, making him jump once more, and again, the quick movement amplifies the pounding in his skull. Tom's strong hand pulls Chris carefully back to the propped-up bed.

"Whoa there, killer. Everything's good. You just cracked your head open a little. The baby is in the nursery, and Cecilia is resting in her own room. They're both perfectly healthy. Nothing to worry about. They brought you to this room to monitor ya cause you got a pretty good concussion, and you were saying some crazy shit, man!" Tom chuckles.

Somehow, the sincerity and paternal concern in Tom's voice is settling. Chris tries to reassure himself that if both Tom and Decker saw the baby, the nightmare from the delivery room had to be a hallucination brought on by fainting and a concussion.

Hoping for a look of confirmation, Chris turns back to Decker. Decker rubs at his wrist and stands at a timid distance from the bed.

"Yeah, man. You were talking about drones and lasers and invisible babies and shit. It was awesome!" Decker's worried look fades, and he laughs with Tom.

The door opens, and Kent backs through it, clumsily dropping straws, napkins, and ketchup packets from a tipped-over fast-food bag atop a mound of other fast-food bags in his arms. Decker, Chris, and Tom stop their conversation to watch Kent fumbling into the room. He begins rambling before he turns around to see them.

"Hey, I wasn't sure what you guys would want, and Christian was out-cold, and his day has been stressful enough, so I wanted to make sure I got something he would like, so I stopped at a couple of different places." He turns and realizes that Chris is now awake. "Oh, hey, Chris. Good to see you're awake. Anyway, my point is, I'm sorry it took so long, but there are tacos and"—he nods to the arm full of bags.

Decker sneers, shakes his head, and rudely snatches a bag. Chris laughs, knowing Decker is just messing with Kent.

Kent cautiously continues—"and some burgers and some Chinese"—

While Kent finishes the list of foods, Tom walks around the

foot of the bed. Without addressing Kent in any way, he gives the mountain of bags a once-over and pulls an oblong bag with a crude graphic of a submarine sandwich on it from the pile.

—"and a couple other things." Kent looks at Tom's selection, "Ah, Carson's Corned Beef. Excellent choice! Is it all right if I set these down over here, Chris? I mean, I can just hold them if you prefer, or, like, leave or whatever."

"It's fine, Kent. Set them down over there."

Kent's erratically paced talking and neurotic questioning is a welcomed distraction from the flashes of the horrific images playing in Chris's head.

"You're sure it's cool if I stay? I could just as easily hang out in the waiting room." He drops the remainder of the bags onto a small end table.

"Christ, Kent!" Decker raises his voice through a mouthful of cheeseburger and fries. "He said it's fine. Shut the fuck up!"

"Okay. Yeah. Cool. I'll just..." Kent's words trail off as he happily mutters to himself and sits in a chair next to Tom.

Halfway through his sandwich and chewing the first bite of the second half, Tom is stopped by Kent, staring at him with a weird smile.

"What?" Tom growls with corned beef and lettuce falling out of his open mouth.

Kent leans slightly toward him. "Yummy, right?"

Tom swallows harshly and wipes his mouth. "Yeah, can you look, like, anywhere else?"

"Sure thing." He redirects his attention back to Chris, who quietly laughs. "So, how are you? Do you need anything? More pillows or something to drink?"

"I'm good, Kent. The food is perfect. I had some twisted fucking dreams, and I have a bit of a headache now, but I'm good."

"Oh, awesome!" He lets out an audible, whew sound of relief. "We were all super worried about you."

Chris smiles, "Thanks, Kent. I appreciate your concern."

"I wasn't worried about you." Decker noisily sucks on the straw of his soda.

They both look at Decker. Kent shakes his head with disapproval while Decker shoves the last bite of his burger into his mouth. His cheek bulges on one side of his face while he chews and speaks out of the other side.

"What? You're fine! He's fine. The doctor said you could get out of here as soon as you woke up." He swallows the generous bite of the burger, which he couldn't have had time enough to chew, and he chases it with another obnoxiously loud sip of his almost empty soda. "She is insanely hot, by the way. Our doctor was a hideous old dude." His head shakes with disappointment. "Anyway, you got a couple of stitches and a mild concussion, no big deal. He said it happens all the time." He balls up his cheeseburger wrapper and tosses it at a trash can in the corner, missing impressively. "Now get up and get dressed, so we can celebrate with these Cubans that Tom was kind enough to bring along." Decker pulls a handful of cigars out of the breast pocket of his jacket and presents them to everyone.

Tom nods and snaps a cigar cutter between his thumb and middle finger while Decker continues.

"And we can—"

"Go see Cecilia and the baby?" Kent timidly interrupts.

Decker rolls his eyes. "Yeah, Kent! We can go see the baby and Cecilia too."

"Let's go outside first." Chris pulls his shirt down over his face. "I could use a little air."

He's sure that what he saw wasn't real, but he is still relieved for the opportunity to stall before seeing the baby again.

.   .   .

"I can't believe I passed out. I'm such an asshole."

"Ah, don't worry. It's like Decker said, it happens all the time." Tom lights his cigar and holds out the torch for Chris and Decker to use.

Chris waves off the light and pulls the cigar out of his mouth. "Nah, I'm good. My head's already spinning."

"Yeah, Christian. Five percent of all new fathers faint during the delivery process," Kent adds.

Decker stares at Kent with pure disdain. "Kent, why do you know that?"

Kent shrugs his shoulders. "I don't know."

Tom puffs his cigar a few times to set the light, pulls it out of his mouth, and blows out a cloud of smoke. His hands grab the tops of Chris's shoulders. The sidestream smoke burns Chris's eye and causes him to choke for a moment.

"Chris, I've been meaning to tell you something my daddy said to me right before Jules and I had our first. I forgot to before, but I think God is giving me a second chance to steer you right since you haven't really seen the kid yet."

Chris's guts twist at Tom's hauntingly accurate words. Tom releases Chris's shoulders, and with his cigar still dangling between his knuckles, he lightly presses his finger to Chris's chest.

"Listen, when you see that baby, it's gonna be ugly. They all are." He hangs and shakes his head, looking down at the ground between them in prayer. "Lord! I tell you, I don't know what it is." He looks back up into Chris's eyes. "It's just nature's way, maybe. Maybe it's to keep other animals from wanting to steal it. I don't claim to know all the answers. All five of mine came out looking like blotchy, slime-covered props from *The Evil Dead*. I swear to God! They're all gorgeous products of my loins now, but they weren't always like that."

Kent, Decker, and Chris all stare at him, speechless.

Tom takes another drag of the stogie, adding to the pungent cloud around him, and continues, "But listen. No matter what. You gotta look right at that hideous creature and then look right into Cecilia's eyes and tell her that thing looks like a goddamn angel. I'm not joking, man. She can't think that you think that baby is ugly, not for a second. She'll never forgive ya. That's why my parents got divorced. My dad swears it."

Chris flinches as Tom slaps his shoulder encouragingly.

For a moment, they all stand silently in disbelief, Tom, allowing for his advice to sink in, the rest, digesting or rightfully trying to forget what they just heard.

Chris reaches out to Tom and pats his shoulder. "Wow! Thanks for that, Tom. That was... truly special. I will not forget that. I don't think any of us will."

Decker and Kent both shake their heads.

"This is a hospital!"

The guys turn their heads toward the security guard's voice behind them.

"Yeah, and?" Decker responds.

"You can't smoke out here." She points to the sizable no-smoking sign on the wall behind them. "You can go across the street, or I can escort you there." She points in the other direction, and their eyes track with her hand to a bus stop across the street. A frail, older woman sits by herself on the bus stop bench. Clear tubing hangs from her nose to an oxygen tank on the ground next to her. Oversized, protective sunglasses cover most of her withered face. A long cigarette dangles from her thin lips.

Tom cringes at the sight of the older woman. "Jesus!"

"All right. Take it easy. Just having a little celebration here." Decker holds his hands up as if he's being arrested. "We'll just put them right in here, OK?" He and Tom drop their cigars into the smoker's receptacle at the edge of the walkway.

Walking back into the hospital, Decker whispers to Chris, "Do you think he realizes his dad was implying he was an ugly baby?"

"Not a chance," Chris responds.

.　　.　　.

At the door to Cecilia's recovery room, Chris pauses with the same hesitant anxiety he suffers when he opens his front door at home when he knows Tom will be waiting for him. *The only things in that room are your wife and your beautiful new daughter. There aren't any weird drones,* he tells himself. He takes a deep breath and turns the door handle. As the door opens, he can immediately hear the buzzing whir of the propeller blades. The drone hovers over Cecilia and the bed.

"Oh, hey, honey! How are you? Look, she's already latching! Oh, my goodness! Look at your poor head. You must feel awful."

He does feel awful, but now there is no way to express what he's truly feeling. Tom's words replay in Chris's brain as it fills with the pressure of rushing blood and deafening pain, *"No matter what. You gotta look right at that hideous creature and then look right into Cecilia's eyes and tell her that thing looks like a goddamn angel."*

Cecilia's breast peeks out of her robe. Her nipple is covered by a suction cup at the end of a mechanical arm coming out of the top of the drone. Over the whir of the propellers, there is a rhythmic, motorized pump noise. A clear telescoping reservoir hangs from the bottom of the drone, slowly filling with milk.

"Christian, are you OK? You're not going to faint again, are you?"

She cradles a small blanket with a tiny knit hat under her breast.

Jesus fucking Christ, I have lost my mind, Chris silently confirms his fear to himself.

Cecilia looks down at the blanket where Chris's eyes are glued.

"Isn't she the most beautiful thing you've ever seen?"

Chris's face is as expressionless and pale as a Roman marble statue. He convinces himself to speak the only words present anywhere in his mind. "She's an angel."

"Aw! Isn't it beautiful, the natural splendor of a mother providing sustenance to a wonderful new life?" From behind Chris in the doorway, Kent wipes a tear from the corner of his eye.

Chris turns around sharply.

"Kent! What the fuck, dude? Get out of here."

Kent smiles under Chris's hand as it mashes his face out of the door.

"What is wrong with you?" He pulls his hand from Kent's face and closes the door into it.

"It's perfectly natural and beautiful, Christian. She shouldn't feel the need to hide it." Kent's voice trails off down the hall.

Cecilia laughs, absolutely unconcerned with Kent having seen most of her breast.

"Come here and meet Evelyn."

The suction cup pulls away from Cecilia's nipple and retracts into the drone. She carefully pulls her robe over her chest.

"Do you want to hold her?"

"You know, maybe it would be best if I don't hold her yet. I'm still a little shaky." He points to the bandage on his head.

His hand reaches out to the empty area where he can only assume Cecilia is seeing a baby. He tickles at the blanket with a gentle touch, emulating how he's seen others interacting with babies that existed.

"Hey there, Evelyn. How are you?" He whispers with his most effeminate voice. He's never felt more confused or ridiculous in his life. There isn't a logical explanation he can imagine for not being able to see a child like everyone else. His thoughts continue to torture him. *This is fucking insane! It must be the concussion. It's got to be! But I saw it before I hit my head. Tom drugged me again. This is all a fucked-up acid trip.*

When Cecilia looks up at him between fawning over the vacant swaddle in her arms, he smiles and tilts his head the way he saw Kent react the first time he held Maya after she was born.

What else do people do? What do men who can actually see their children usually say? he pleads with his memory to come up with anything.

"You did such an amazing job, honey. She's perfect." A piercing ringing screams through his head, disorienting him and deadening his other senses. He pets Cecilia's shoulder with a firm assuring hand and does his best to ignore the drone hovering above them.

His body stiffens at the sight of a metal tube snaking down into the baby blanket. Looking up at the drone, he sees another metal arm reach over into the drain in the sink. The milk in the reservoir disappears and retracts into the bottom of the drone.

"Oh! I think she's wet. Evie's first diaper change." Tears gather in her eyes as she laughs. "Ha, ha, who would have ever thought a person could be this happy because someone else peed!"

Chris grabs at the back of his aching neck.

"Yeah, pretty crazy, right?" He does his best imitation of a laugh while reaching for the pain pills in his pocket.

15. Back to Work

Chris turns the key to the off position and pulls it from the steering column. The car responds with delayed sputtering and shaking as the engine dies. He's late, noticeably late. He leans back into the headrest, closes his eyes, and forces himself to breathe deeply. No one will say anything about his punctuality, especially since he has a newborn at home. He's aware of this, but a hint of the old anxiety of being late to work still lingers enough to make him feel shitty about it.

Thoughts of glad-handing friends and relatives at the hospital claw at the disintegrating fabric of his sanity. His face still hurts from the cramp-inducing fake smile he's been forcing since the... it... thing... whatever was born. He doesn't know what to call the baby. When he tries to say she or Evelyn in a conversation, he stutters every time. The muscles in his cheeks can finally relax, here, in his car, without the rest of the world staring at him, waiting to hear every detail about the baby. There is nothing he can say without internally wishing for his own quick death. This procrastination in the car will be his only reprieve. As soon as he steps into the office, it will be, *"Oh my God! How did everything go? You must be so excited! Can we see a picture?"* There is a picture to show them. It gets the same excited reactions from everyone—*"Absolutely adorable!"*, *"She's so precious!"*, *"She looks just like her mamma!"*, *"She's like a mini-*

you, Chris!" or one of the more annoying versions—*"How did YOU make that?"*, *"Good thing she takes after her mother!"* Chris sees none of this. When he looks at the photo, he sees an exhausted Cecilia still bright with a happy, postnatal glow. In her arms, there is a blanket loosely wrapped around itself and a pink beanie. Where there should be a precious, squishy, little baby face, there is only something that resembles what television static looks like when he's not wearing his contacts. He wishes everyone would just shut the fuck up about the goddamn baby. He wishes, more than anything, that he could see what they say they're seeing. Being reminded that he can't, when it's the only thing he can think about already, is infuriating.

He glances down at his hands. They're trembling with anxiety and anger. He clenches them into fists and opens them, extending his fingers as far as possible. Quickly, he repeats the process a couple more times, but it doesn't help steady them.

Leaning his head back, he turns his face to look through his window and across the street at the O.K. Package building. The architecture of the ten-story office building is as mundane as everything happening inside it. He is bored at the sight of it, and he's felt this way since he can remember, yet today, it is more welcoming than he ever imagined possible. Even during the depths of Cecilia's depression, regardless of how taxing it was to be at home, he still preferred being home to being here. Now, after a few weeks of being in a house with that thing and having to pretend he sees what Cecilia sees, the possibility of spending nine hours listening to Kent's nervous stammering and Paula's flirty, rhyming, disingenuous salutations sounds like a reprieve. Even if he is accosted and interrogated about all things baby for the first few hours, it'll still be better.

As he reaches back for his shoulder bag, his eye catches the familiar fluorescent orange rims of the flipped-up, Wayfarer sunglasses that the strange man was wearing at Tyler's birthday party over nine months ago. The man is sitting on the bus stop bench outside the O.K. Package entrance. Chris pushes his door open and stands next to his car, squinting and trying to decide if it is, in fact, the same guy. He isn't certain. The man is looking down, scribbling in a book, but the glasses are definitely the same. Chris can't be one hundred percent sure from this distance, but it appears that aside from the brown sports coat now added to the ensemble, the man is also wearing the same swim trunks, flip-flops, and t-shirt that the man was wearing when Chris first saw him at Tyler's birthday party. He unconsciously whispers to himself his now most common and repetitive thought, "What the fuck?"

By the time he is halfway across the street, Chris can tell that this is the same man and the same clothes. Chris cannot help himself from blatantly gawking. As he passes the bench, he realizes how long he's been staring and forces himself to turn his head toward the front door of the office. A nasal and accusatory voice chirps from behind him.

"You can see me."

The scrawny man tilts his book down and picks up his head as Chris turns to the sound of the man's voice. The man continues to look straight ahead. Chris steps toward the bench.

"What? Are you talking to me?"

The man folds his book under his arm and looks at Chris's face. "You can see me, can't you?" He smacks his leg and stands before Chris can respond to the question. "Well, of course, you can! You saw me at the party, and you're seeing me right now."

"Um, yeah, I can see you."

The man smiles but awkwardly tries to hold his lips together. His teeth peek through despite his attempts to conceal them. He wags his finger at Chris.

"I knew it!"

Chris waits for the man to say something else, but the man adds nothing. He only smiles and stares back at Chris.

Chris breaks the awkward silence.

"Well, I have to go to work now."

He gestures toward the office door and turns away from the stranger, positive that he has completely lost his mind. Even this amount of weirdness seems almost standard at this point. *"Of course! As if fathering a drone-baby wasn't enough. Now I have to deal with this freaky asshole? Sure. Yeah. Why not?"* Chris's brain yells at him. Pulling the door open, he is able to muster what he knows will be a fleeting sense of relief, considering how much more out of his mind this man must be than he is himself.

"Okay, we'll talk more soon. Good luck in there, friend."

"God, I hope not! Good luck in there? What the fuck is that supposed to mean?" Chris's thoughts shout inside of his mind again. The man's wish felt oddly genuine, which made it even more disconcerting. Confused and looking back over his shoulder at the man, he shuffles through the door.

"Uh, thanks. I guess."

The door closes behind him. He shakes off the encounter as he walks through the empty lobby to the elevator.

"What the fuck?" he whispers to himself, alone inside the elevator. The ding of the elevator door reaching his floor cuts off his darting thoughts. Remembering how late he is and hoping to avoid eye contact with anyone else today, he looks down at his feet and steps out onto his floor. He turns the corner out of the elevator bay to the empty reception desk. No one is there to exchange monotonous pleasantries with him. This rare lack of interaction from the lobby to his cubicle comforts him immensely. There is no telling how long he could pretend he's been here without anyone noticing. He slinks around the end of the line of cubicles, passes Kent's, and ducks into his own. His bag falls from his shoulder onto the cheap, carpet-square-covered floor. Inside his cubicle, there's only an empty desk and chair. He looks up and over the partitions. Each cubicle is the same—an empty chair, an empty desk, no computers, no pens, no Kent twitching, no one, nothing anywhere.

There is only a faint sound of machinery. Chris cautiously walks in the direction of the noise, past the reception desk and elevators. The noise grows as he approaches the stairwell. He pushes through the door, and the volume doubles. The stairwell railing vibrates against his hand while he descends the three flights of stairs to the shipping and receiving warehouse catwalk door, where the machine noise is loudest. He can make out the faint voices of a crowd mixed in with the racket. The calamity surges as he opens the door and walks onto the catwalk. Except for the intermittent beeping of a forklift in reverse and the chuckling of a few workers after a dirty joke, this cavernous room is usually quiet. Chris looks down from the catwalk onto a clustered maze of equipment he doesn't recognize at all. There are hydraulic, robotic contraptions manufacturing parts on conveyor belts lined with his coworkers in hard hats. Paula's shrill voice cuts through the chatter, the echoing whir of the machinery, and the plastic snapping of drone components locking together.

"Okie Dokie, Artichokie!"

As he walks down the steps, he can see Kent near the end of the belt, moving finished drone-babies from the line and packing them into O.K. Package packages. Usually, these are only filled with other O.K. Package's packaging materials to be shipped to other companies who use them to package and ship their actual products. Chris's airways tighten with panic. He steps onto the warehouse floor and approaches Kent.

"Kent, what the fuck is going on, man?"

Kent's eyes are fixed on the drones. With his face completely blank of any emotion, he begins to whisper, "I'm going to go to the bathroom. Can you cover for me?" This is something he's said to Chris a million times, but this time, he isn't asking Chris. To Chris, it doesn't seem as though Kent is actually speaking to anyone in particular.

"Dude, what are you doing? What the fuck are you talking about?"

Kent is silent and continues to move the drones into boxes.

Decker walks past them to the filled boxes and begins to tape them closed. His eyes are as still and focused as Kent's.

"We gotta cut outta here, man! I need a drink or something." Decker's words are directed at no one. His eyes blankly stare past Chris into the dark corners of the warehouse. Chris puts his hand on Decker's shoulder.

"Are you OK, man?"

"C'mon, Chris! I just saw Jackhole go into the shitter with his phone. He's good for at least half an hour in there, and then he's going to lunch. Besides, he hasn't freaked out on anyone since Darkest Day. We are all good until at least one o'clock."

Decker continues sealing the boxes. This is more work than Chris has seen him do in years. It may be more work than he's done in his entire life. Chris realizes Decker is repeating his side of a conversation they had more than nine months ago, the day Decker told him about Building Blocks Labs.

"Oh, hey, Paula! Lovely to see you. Have a lovely day!"

Paula shouts from off in the distance, "You fir-irst!"

"Un-fucking-real!" Chris says to himself as he steps back away from Decker.

"What? I just said, 'Hello!'"

Decker pauses while Chris recalls his part of the conversation and whispers it to himself. "Yeah, I heard. It was lovely!"

Without looking at Chris, Decker continues, "Dude, do you want to cut out of here or not?"

"Oh, hey guys," Kent chimes in on cue.

Decker and Kent continue to mindlessly pack and seal boxes of drone-babies while repeating the conversation, word for word, about Kent almost falling in the shower. Chris's mind flashes back and forth from the day they first had the conversation to now.

Decker stops sealing boxes. "C'mon, man! Let's go," he says as he hands the tape gun and hard hat to Kent. He turns and walks toward the main office lobby. Stupefied, Chris follows him into the main lobby and out through the front door. They stop on the sidewalk next to the bench where the man with the orange glasses was sitting. The man is no longer anywhere in sight. Decker pulls a cigarette out of his pocket, lights it, and turns to Chris.

"Dude, thanks. I had to get the fuck out of there."

"Are you talking to me?" Chris can feel his mouth hanging open. He looks directly into Decker's now lucid eyes.

"Why the fuck are you looking at me like that?" Decker sneers, speaking out of one side of his mouth while the other grips his bouncing cigarette.

"You're talking to me now?"

"Uh, yeah! Who the fuck else would I be talking to?" He pulls his Marlboro from his lips and blows out two lungfuls of smoke as he speaks, "You OK, man? You look like hell! You're not having a fucking stroke, are you?"

"I don't know, maybe." Chris seriously considers the question.

"C'mon, let's go get a drink. You'll feel better."

16. Who Needs a Drink

Chris stares, perplexed and mute, at Decker ordering their drinks.

"I'll have my usual and a Manhattan for m'lady?"

Decker looks at Chris to confirm the order. Chris continues to stare blankly back at him. How can this Decker be the same expressionless, lobotomized person who was, mere minutes ago, mindlessly taping boxes in the O.K. Package warehouse? It doesn't make sense. Decker should have been doing what he always does at work, standing at his desk, passively accepting the advances of horny, baby-obsessed, female office employees.

"Do you want a Manhattan?"

Decker points at the bartender. Chris looks at the attractive woman behind the bar. She waits for his response. He can only stare in dazed silence as her look of impatient bewilderment grows. She raises her eyebrows, glances back at Decker, and nods questioningly.

"Chris, Manhattan?" Decker asks again.

"Ah, no!" Chris is startled back to reality and addresses the bartender directly, "I'll just have a beer or whatever he's having."

"Yeah, good choice," she mocks him.

With an air of annoyance and without needing to look at what she's doing, she spins her bottle opener, opens two bottles of beer, slides the bottle opener back into a sweatband on her forearm, and pushes the beer across the bar to them. Both her irritation and mechanics suggest she has done this thousands of times for thousands of indecisive customers. There is a jaded elegance and distinct boredom in each movement of her precise technique. For this part of her vocation, she wastes no amount of energy on thought. She negotiates the basic tediums of her job with an automated, mechanical muscle memory that is as natural and as effortless as breathing.

"What's with you, man? Baby keeping you up all night? Man, I don't miss that shit. Maya's been sleeping straight through the night, finally. Thank God!"

"Yeah, maybe I'm just tired." Chris tries to convince himself, though he knows he has no hope that any of this is due to a little sleep deprivation.

"You just gotta give them a routine, you know? They're like little machines. They just need to be programmed to sleep when you do and eat—"

Chris's internal dialogue drowns out Decker's voice.

"Yeah, exactly. Little fucking machines are what they are. This is it. I full-on lost my fucking mind. None of this can be fucking real, can it?"

Tuning back in on Decker's voice, Chris realizes he has no idea what Decker has been saying.

"—right there in the fucking parking lot. I'm not saying do it every day, but fuck, man, everybody needs to shut it down every now and then."

"What?" Chris asks.

He desperately tries to pay attention to Decker's response, but all Chris can think of is sitting in the dark nursery staring at the blinking red light and listening to the hum of the four propellers on his drone-baby. He can hear every word Decker says, but none of it computes.

"Leave early for work and take a nap in the parking lot. Hell, I used to do it way before I even had a kid. Fuck, do it on your way out of work too. Hell, sometimes I book the conference rooms for fake meetings. I just go in, close the door, and fucking sleep across a few chairs. You should give it a shot."

"Yeah, a shot. A shot sounds good." Chris rubs his eyes.

"Fuck yeah, it does! That's my boy. Bartender, two shots of your finest mid-shelf, under-ten-dollar bourbon for me and my friend here."

She grabs a bottle from the shelf and saunters toward them.

"Ooh, big spender!"

She pours the liquor into two shot glasses.

"My man, right here, he's a new daddy! We are celebrating and commiserating."

Her attitude straightens, and the sarcasm falls from her tone.

"Really? Wow! That's great! Congratulations! Shots are on the house, but let's break out something more appropriate than this swill."

She turns to grab a bottle from the top shelf.

Decker leans into Chris, "See, it certainly has its perks. Trust me, though. It gets old after a while."

Leaving the already-poured shots on the bar, the bartender cracks three more shot glasses onto the bar top and fills them with the high-end liquor. "Enjoy your shots, boys." She grins seductively at Chris as she downs her shot and walks away.

Joseph D. Newcomer

"Would you look at that shit? Way too young and totally out of your league, but now that she knows you have the goods, none of that matters to her."

"Christ, is this all you think about?" He turns to Decker, who is now staring at the bartender's ass."

"Um, actually, yeah, and to tell you the truth, it's a bit of a curse. I think about having sex with everyone I see. Hell, I'm imagining having a threesome with you and that bartender right now." Decker points his chin at the bartender.

The bartender tries to watch them out of the corner of her eye. She helps the next person at the bar, but she's eavesdropping on their conversation. Chris notices her, and she flashes him a smile and turns away.

Chris turns to Decker. "You really are deranged. You know that, right?"

"You'll find out. You don't understand now, but you will. When it's in your face all day, every day, it warps your mind."

"Please, never make me think of being in a threesome with you and anyone else ever again."

"Fair enough," Decker concedes.

"Decker, what were you doing at work?"

"What do you mean? Same shit I do every day, as little as fucking possible." Decker laughs at his own joke and sips his beer.

"Were you in the warehouse at all today?" He tries to coax Decker into some sort of recollection of packaging drone-babies for mass distribution.

"What? Why the fuck would I go to the warehouse? I was with you the whole morning. We walked over here together. When would I have gone to the warehouse? Wait, is Ed in the warehouse

118

selling that killer Kush again?" Decker's eyes light up at the thought of the weed. "Shit! Are you holding?"

"What? No! You don't remember anything else out of the ordinary?"

Decker shrugs his shoulders. "Ah, no, not really. You mean, besides the way you're acting right now? No, nothing out of the ordinary. Seriously, are you all right, man?"

Chris stands, tips his first shot into his mouth, and picks up the second as he forces the first down his throat. He puts the second to his mouth and drinks it while he sets the first empty glass back on the bar. Decker sarcastically holds his first shot out to cheers with no one and drinks it.

"I have to go, man. I... I'll see you tomorrow." Chris turns and walks toward the door.

Decker raises his voice to Chris's back. "Hey, I was kidding, man, about the threesome. Kind of."

The bar chatter goes quiet as Chris stops to look back at Decker. Several other customers turn their heads to look over their shoulders at Chris, standing near the doorway. Chris raises his hands as if to say, what the fuck? The people at the bar turn their heads to follow Chris's disapproving eyes back to Decker. Decker scans the line of judgmental faces. His nostrils flare with annoyance as he addresses everyone in the bar, "What? Like none of you assholes ever wanted to have a threesome? I'm the only degenerate in the whole bar?"

The other patrons sheepishly look back to their drinks. Chris turns and continues to the door. Decker holds out his second shot in Chris's direction as he leaves.

"OK, pal. Nice talk. Cheers!" He swallows the liquor and shouts more loudly, cupping his hand to his mouth to project his words to Chris at the front door of the bar. "Oh, hey, remember what

I said! Dad-life is all about naps, man. You can probably grab one right now before you go home."

The door closes behind Chris.

17. Who's the Man

Relieved to be home, Chris pulls into the driveway. The shots of bourbon kick in, mildly sedating his concern for his sanity. He sighs along with the death rattle of the Corolla's seizing engine as he reaches for the loose driver's door latch.

"I bet—" The nasal voice of the man with the orange sunglasses startles Chris.

"What the"—Chris flings the door open and tries to jump from the vehicle. He finishes his sentence as he trips over the door frame and his own feet and falls, face-first, onto the cement driveway—"fuck!"

He scrambles to his feet. The man calmly opens the rear door and steps out of the car.

"Why the fuck are you in my car? Who the fuck are you? Why are you following me around?"

Startled, Chris backs away defensively.

"I bet this all must be pretty strange to you?" The odd man giggles and snorts the same way he did at the children playing in the pool at Tyler's party.

"Strange? Yeah, that may be the understatement of the fucking century!"

The man's voice adopts the tone of a scolding grandparent. "First of all, you know you really shouldn't drink and drive. That is extremely dangerous. Also, you are aware that your cracked rearview mirror is lying on the floor in the back seat. You would have noticed me much sooner had it been where it should be. I'm seriously concerned with your driving safety choices."

"Yeah, I'll take that under advisement as soon as you tell me what the fuck you were doing in my car in the first place!" Chris pulls the car door open and reaches for his phone but doesn't take his eyes off the man.

"In good time. You can put your phone away. You don't need to contact the authorities. I assure you, you are in no danger. For now, though, let's go inside. Do you see how Tom is looking at you?"

The man points to Tom in the next yard. Brushing himself off from the fall, Chris looks to see Tom's staring, confused face. Behind Tom, his front door opens. Julia steps onto the porch, and a small drone follows her through the door. Her upper body is angled as if she is holding something, something about the size of her nearly three-year-old daughter. Julia cradles an empty blanket to her side with one hand while her other hand caresses the air where the child should be. She smiles and waves to Chris. Tom lets go of the hedge trimmer throttle to give an awkward half-wave as well. Chris nods and pensively waves back to the couple.

"Tom cannot see me. Right now, as Tom perceives it, you are standing out here talking to yourself. I think it would be best if we went inside your house to continue our conversation. I'll explain everything. Let's calm down and go inside."

The man reaches for Chris's elbow and guides him to turn around. They walk together to the front door. Chris unlocks and opens the door while looking over his shoulder at Tom and his giant exposed teeth. Tom and his teeth stare back in utter confusion.

The man politely folds his hands together in front of him and enters the house. He steps to the side of the door, grins, and looks around.

"You have a lovely home."

The man's calm presence and relaxed state only intensify Chris's agitation and confusion.

"Thanks."

"You're welcome. Hi, I'm Lester."

He extends his bony hand to Chris.

"Hi."

Chris shakes the man's hand and waivers between docile, helpless confusion and rage.

What are you doing here? Why were you in my car and outside of my job? Why the fuck did you wish me good luck? Do you have something to do with what's going on in there?"

"I'll answer all of your questions. First, let me ask you, are you concerned at all about the future, Christian?"

"Not until fucking today, Lester!"

"Ha, humor! Splendid! What a wonderfully natural response to a crisis. I do so enjoy your delightfully sardonic nature, Chris. However, I would truly like you to consider the question. Do you still have any conception of our impending doom as a society? I mean, apart from what I'm assuming you saw at work today and your visual interpretation of your child, which I can only assume must be highly upsetting to you. Aside from these recent terrors, were you at all troubled by thoughts of civilization ending?" Lester pauses and waits for Chris to respond.

Chris considers the question but shrugs his shoulders in defeat.

"Is the answer, 'No?' I don't know. Maybe? Kind of tough to honestly consider that particular question at this point. You know, since I assume I'm having some sort of manic episode or something."

"OK. Let us assume that you were not having those types of thoughts before and that we can safely agree that you are of average or greater intelligence and tend to be logical with an inclination for forethought typical of a person with your level of deductive acumen. Fair?"

Chris senses absolutely no condescension in Lester's voice, yet he can't help but feel as though Lester is speaking down to him from the pedestal of a much higher IQ.

"Sure, what the fuck!"

"You really are quite funny." Lester cackles again.

"Thanks, I guess."

"I'll get right to it. And please understand, I would not tell you this unless I was certain that within moments from now, even without my prompting, you would come to this knowledge all on your own. With all these things taken into account—"

Chris drops to the chair at his kitchen table, interrupting Lester with epiphanic expletives. "Holy fucking shit! The world is over. That's what you're going to say, isn't it?"

The thoughts connect in Chris's mind while he runs his hands and arms over his table. The smooth varnish-coated, wooden surface is cold and soothing. His posture sinks into his seat. He stares in the direction of his hands, sweeping over the wood grain of the table, but really, at nothing.

"Yes, I believe I exceeded the time in which I had to explain myself. My apologies. I can be terribly verbose at times, and I was excited to meet you. But yes, what you have, no doubt, just realized is that humanity has a finite amount of time left. The children are not real. None of them are. Even if they were, at the rate children are believed to be being conceived, we couldn't possibly sustain a rate of reproduction that would allow us to exist for much longer anyway. The actuality is, as I said, none of the children born since Darkest Day are real. As you, no doubt, are working out in your mind, humanity has no more than a hundred years left as that's when the youngest of us will die, give or take a few years. Probably more take than give considering our now greatly declining, true life expectancy."

Chris looks up from the table and at Lester. Lester's expression is plain and empathetic.

"Yeah, no. Thanks. I get it now. Why didn't I—"

"Think of this sooner?" Lester interrupts. "Yes, that is the next logical and glaringly human question. The answer is distraction, suggestion, and a small, almost negligible, amount of drugging and mind control."

Lester holds his index finger and thumb in front of his eye. He looks through the small gap between his fingers to indicate to Chris just how insignificant of an amount of drugging and mind control was being used to stave off the widespread panic that public knowledge of the apocalypse would cause.

"A small amount of drugging and mind control! What in the fuck is that supposed to mean?"

"Well, it wouldn't have done any good to have people figure out the glaringly obvious fact that with no new procreation to speak of, we would quickly cease to exist." Lester takes the seat across from Chris, who is a statue of horror and disbelief, sitting at the kitchen table. "No, that would have brought back the rioting and mass hysteria, which I found extremely unpleasant."

"Yeah, it was a real drag."

"Yes, I know. I couldn't agree more." Lester completely misses Chris's sarcasm. "So, I decided we would begin covertly releasing a sort of anti-anxiety, calm-inducing chemical compound into the atmosphere while we filtered out the more dangerous chemicals and pollutants. When everyone's sense of fear was dampened, everything was immediately easier to handle."

"Who the fuck is 'we?'" Do you work for Retsel and Beta Sciences?"

A few weeks ago, Chris would have stopped this conversation well before they went into his house. After seeing his drone-baby and everyone at work today, he will entertain any explanation.

"Please, Christian! Retsel, Lester, I mean, come on! You're certainly more intelligent than that. I know this for a fact. He is an automaton, a cyborg. I created him to be the face of Beta. There is no Retsel. It's just Lester—me—Retsel spelled backward. Get it?"

"You? You saved the entire planet from certain destruction by drugging everyone? Fucking Tom is going to love this. Why did you make up Retsel?"

"In a word, yes. I assure you that everything was much more complicated than that, but yes, for our purposes, I saved the world. Studies showed that people would more readily accept someone with certain physical attributes as a leader. People aren't entirely comfortable being led by someone they view as physically inferior, regardless of their intellect. A strong chin goes a long way. It also frees me from the obligations of public life."

"Fantastic! And anti-anxiety medication kept everyone from realizing we're going extinct?" Chris raises and flops his hands onto the table. He wishes he wasn't believing this.

"Well, not just that. And again, it's far more complicated than this, but the airborne anxiolytics and, I assure you, very mild tranquilizers make everyone a little more open to suggestion. The mood enhancers and stabilizers are accompanied by subliminal messages carried over infra and ultrasonic frequencies that we continuously broadcast through any sound transmitting device—everything from television and radio stations to crosswalk speakers. Your cell phone emits the frequencies even when you're not using it. You probably noticed that the effect bleeds mildly into other aspects of your daily life as well. Not everyone is in tune with it, but perhaps you're a little less concerned about some things that you remember having a deeper impact on your psyche previously. Maybe you noticed a positive change in the more aggressive types of people around you. All in all, even the side effects have been overwhelmingly positive."

"Actually, yeah. That makes a lot of sense. What about work, though? What about the freaky fucking drone-babies?" Chris asks.

"Christian, I really don't care for it when you refer to them that way," Lester admonishes him with a look of parental disappointment.

"OK! What would make you think I might give a fuck, Lester?"

Lester ignores this question and moves on to answering the previous ones.

"The facade of normalcy requires everyone's assistance. The way I see it, we all benefit from it, so we should all play a role in doing the work to keep it going. Your coworkers and, until recently, you were experiencing your workdays on a three-month loop. The delicate and quite ingenious, I might add, toot, toot"—Lester raises his hand and pulls down on an imaginary trolley whistle— "subliminal suggestions are layered, allowing your conscious mind to perceive your own stored memories of your day's interactions while your subconscious guides your physical movements to complete a program of tasks. The tasks provide the means that allow us to continue our new way of life. Your business manufactures the Sentient Infantile Stereopticons while—"

"You mean, the drone-babies?"

Lester closes his eyes to recover his patience and continues.

"—while another business may be processing the medicament to be released into the air or ensuring that the digital and analog broadcast signals are at optimal quality. The Sentient Infantile Stereopticons, don't!"—he holds his hand up to stop Chris, who was preparing to, once again, correct Lester's terminology. Chris sighs and allows him to continue.—"project perfectly compelling imagery directly into the eyes or the viewable perception of their surrogate parents as well as any other bystanders who are present. They also emit their own individual infra and ultrasonic frequencies. These subliminal messages convince our senses to believe that we are not only visually experiencing a fully realized child but also that the visual representation of the child is affecting us in every other perceivable way. Additionally, they transmit a digital signal in the event they are being surveilled, or, you know, for family pictures. It can be a little trickier for analog photography, but I digress. We use parental DNA to calculate their simulated offspring's physical and mental traits. From those calculations, we create a unique program for each SIS. Their programs follow the averages according to the DNA for growth, development, temperament, health, and so on. They are virtually indiscernible from an organically created child."

"Well, you did a horrible fucking job because they don't look anything like an actual fucking baby to me!" Chris cannot help but shout.

"Yes, well, as with any system, there are certain anomalies. However, the good news is that I believe I can fix the issue if you would like. I can't force your mind to unlearn what you know, but I can, with a high probability of success, inhibit the specific synaptic connections in your brain, which, for some reason, are fully operational even with the continual dose of anxiolytic drugs and subliminal messaging. It is my opinion, based on several other tests done without your knowledge over the past several weeks, that this is not an issue of your body building a tolerance to the anxiolytic drugs, but we will test for this more extensively in a controlled environment if you are willing to allow it. The best-case scenario, also the least likely, will be that varying the drugs in dosage and type will, once again, inhibit those connections and allow for you to perceive the intended physical appearance and actions of your SIS and all the others. If the drug variance does not work, we can map all the synaptic connections in your brain and surgically inhibit the connections that allow you to see the 'drone-babies' instead of the desired projections. This will take some time, as you may have up to one quadrillion synaptic connections. Worst case scenario, we are unable to find the reason, and you continue to see the world as you do currently."

"Sounds like the worst-case scenario is I die during a brain surgery that may or may not be able to make it so that I can see fake babies and not have panic attacks about humanity's inevitable doom. And regardless of the outcome, I would still know everything I know right now, but I might be able to be sedated enough not to let it ruin my day." Chris watches the slow calculation of his correction playing out in Lester's thoughtful expressions.

Lester rolls his eyes and laughs at his oversight.

"My mistake. Of course! I suppose, from your personal perspective, death would seem like the worst-case scenario. Ha! I hadn't even considered that." The pitch of Lester's voice rises with his unexpected amusement.

"Is it, though? I guess I don't even know anymore." Chris is much less amused than Lester.

"Regardless, I assure you, your death is highly improbable. You needn't worry."

Lester smiles encouragingly, but it has no effect on Chris.

"Well, thanks, weird guy wearing flip-flops who I met today

at a bus stop and who also wants to operate on my brain. I'm so much more at ease. Why did you tell me this? Why didn't you just kidnap me, drug me, and fix the problem? Wouldn't that have solved everything?"

"Apart from that being highly undignified, first, I'm not completely certain we will be successful, and second, for this to work, it is important that you desire for it to work. You would be surprised what people are willing to believe when you show them what they want to see. If you were resistant to it, even if you didn't know what it was that you were resisting, I feared we would have a much lower success rate. If we pursue this, I can't have you wondering what may or may not be going on and why. You must know everything so that you won't be distracted. Everyone else wants to see what they're seeing. This fact makes it easier to show them exactly that. Think about it. Technically, you see exactly what you've always wanted to see. You didn't want a baby, you just wanted Cecilia to be happy, and you've succeeded on both accounts. This also means you won't be as easily convinced by any means."

Chris shakes his head in amazement but has no words. He can only continue to listen. Even his typically wandering mind remains focused on Lester's words. Chris is entirely consumed by the strange and sordid details of a reality that would have been an impossibility to him before his child was snapped together and powered on. Now, all of this is entirely plausible, and there is no need for his mind to create fantasies to entertain him. This insanity is enough to occupy his thoughts fully.

"Synapses in your brain are strengthened with use and decline without it. My theory is that your constant thinking about, imagining, talking about, and worrying about babies, or more specifically not having babies, may have strengthened the connections in those neural pathways enough that when you were presented with a thing that was not a baby, regardless of how well disguised, you were able to see that you, in fact, did not have a baby. I also believe that your hyper-focus on all things baby-related may have distracted you from the subliminal suggestions, ultimately allowing you to see me. Then, of course, you, being entirely consumed with the questioning of your reality and sanity, broke down the rest of the facade, allowing you to see what you hadn't at your work. I observed you from a distance. I knew it was inevitable that you would see everything as it truly is, and I had to allow it. Otherwise, you may not have believed me."

"I guess that makes as much sense as any of this." Chris shrugs.

"I assumed you would opt to try any or all the methods I've explained for the same reason that led you to procure one of our Stereopticons in the first place. Clearly, your happiness is almost entirely dependent on Cecilia's. I surmised that it might be a lot easier for you to keep this information to yourself while retaining some sense of sanity if you were able to see the child as she does."

"What makes you think I won't tell everyone what's going on?"

"I believe I answered that, but even aside from your clear desire to keep Cecilia happy, if you think about it for any amount of time, you will come to realize that sharing this information with everyone simply doesn't benefit anyone. More than likely, you would be seen as an insane person. No one would believe this, and you would have no way of proving it to people because they cannot see what you're seeing. But, simply for the sake of argument, let's assume you are not seen as mentally unstable. How might it benefit you? Except for unloading the burden of knowledge and providing some initial reprieve from your stress, it would be of minimal benefit to anyone. The side effects, as I mentioned, could be mass panic or, perhaps just as catastrophic, abject apathy could befall every living person once they know everything they do will be meaningless, from this point until the end of humanity. Basically, you would be passing your torture to the rest of the world, including Cecilia, negating any relief you may have felt by unburdening your conscience in the first place. Still, the most deciding factor, in my opinion, is that even if nothing adverse happens at all, telling people would serve no purpose. Nothing can be changed. All, if any negative outcomes, would be for not. Nothing we say or do for the next hundred years will—"

"Jesus, man, I get it! So, what now?" He stops Lester. His head pounds, and he just wants the conversation to end.

"Starting tomorrow, if you so choose, you will start and end your days as usual. Get up, say good morning to your wife and child, and go to work. I, or one of my assistants, will be waiting at your office to bring you to the lab. At the end of the day, according to the schedule, which is programmed for your work hours, you will return to the office and proceed as normal."

18. The Makings of a Christian

Chris lets off the gas, and the Corolla stalls, turning into the parking lot across from O.K. Package. The car has enough momentum to coast most of the way into a parking spot. Decker is standing next to his own car in his nearby parking space. As Chris comes to a complete stop, Decker shoves the Corolla the rest of the way into the spot.

"What would you do without me?" Decker gloats as Chris steps out of the car.

"I have no idea how any of us could ever get along without you," Chris answers.

They walk across the street.

"You good, man? You kind of left me hanging last night."

Chris has forgotten all about abruptly leaving the bar. After his discussion with Lester, Chris could only think of the things Lester said. He barely slept, going over and over their conversation all night long.

"Yeah, sorry, I wasn't feeling too well."

"The shits?" Decker nods his head, answering his own question.

"What? No!"

"I get it, man. I hate taking shits in public. They're just not as satisfying. It's like trying to scratch your balls when there are people around. You can wrestle your sac from inside your pocket without raising too many eyebrows, but what can you really do with this?" Decker holds up his hand with his fingers extended and held tightly together. "What the fuck are you supposed to do with a fucking penguin flipper? Every man knows the only way to scratch scrote skin is by pinching"—he makes a pinching motion with his index finger and thumb—"and twisting"—he rubs his pinching fingertips together—"like you're rolling up some snot, so you can toss it."

Chris stops just outside the building and looks at Decker.

"Decker, never touch anything of mine again."

Decker opens the front door and holds it for Chris.

"Fine! Act like you don't know what I'm talking about."

Chris walks by him and into the lobby. As Decker steps through the door frame, his face drains of expression. He turns and walks toward the warehouse.

"Decker?"

Decker doesn't respond. He can't. He's not even really there. Chris watches him turn the corner into the warehouse. A small drone flies through the lobby and stops directly in front of him. The drone is no different from the drone that is supposed to be his child. He stares at its blinking red light.

"Christian," Lester's cheery, nasal voice comes from a speaker on the drone. "Are you ready to begin?"

"Ah, yeah, sure. This isn't weird at all." Chris rubs at the tight muscles in the back of his neck.

"OK then, follow me."

Chris turns as the drone moves around him and flies to the automatic door opener. A probing, robotic antenna reaches out from the drone and gently presses the button. The door opens, and the drone spins back to face Chris.

"After you."

Chris walks outside to find an autonomous car with its door open. The drone flies off in the other direction.

"Well, come on!" Lester leans to look through the open door from the other side of the back seat. He pats the seat and motions for Chris to get in. "Hurry, we'll try to have you back before happy hour."

They sit silently as the car drives itself and them across town. Lester stares out of his window like a child seeing the city for the first time.

Lester turns to Chris as the car comes to a stop. "Go ahead inside. I'm in there waiting for you."

Lester's eyes close, and his head tips down as if he's fallen asleep. The sound of hydraulic pressure releasing comes from somewhere in his body. Chris's door opens. Another drone is there, waiting for him, hanging ominously on nothing in the air.

"It's OK. Don't be shy." Lester's voice comes from the drone again. It backs away from the car, giving Chris enough space to get out.

Chris follows the drone into the imposing glass monument of the Beta Sciences building. The exterior is perfectly transparent. Through the glass, he can see people attending meetings and moving about on every floor. The bulky security guard inside the lobby waves to Chris and the drone as they approach the door. The drone beeps, and the door opens to reveal a vast, bright, almost empty space reminiscent of an airplane hangar. Chris realizes the exterior of the building is only a high-definition video façade. Inside, there is only this room and a few tents in the middle of it. There are no other people, only another Lester walking toward Chris from the center of the massive space. This Lester is wearing a lab coat but still dons his flip-flops and orange Wayfarers with the lenses flipped up. As he comes nearer, he smiles and waves to Chris.

"I trust you found us easily. I hope everyone has been helpful so far this morning."

"Everyone? You mean, drone-you and the other robot-you from the car? Yeah, they were great, not creepy at all. Does anyone else work here?" Chris's raised voice echoes around the titanic indoor stadium.

"Here? Forty-six thousand, six hundred and ninety-two, to be precise, but they work remotely. Of course, there are more working at satellite offices like your O.K. Package, and more, still, at subsidiaries. I guess everyone kind of works here, really, so five billionish, but this is my personal workstation. I only have a few robotic replications of myself that help me on-site, but other than that, no. It's just me."

Lester lowers his voice as Chris comes closer. "They're almost perfect, aren't they? The one you met in the car, you couldn't tell it wasn't me, could you?"

"No, I couldn't. How could I? How could I even know if I'm talking to you now?"

"Well, I guess you couldn't. Not unless you cut me open, I imagine. I guess you'll have to take my word for it." Lester smiles.

.   .   .

"First, we'll do several scans of you for your mannerisms, musculature, and such so that we can create a convincing android in your likeness."

"A fake me, great! This always works so well in the movies."

Lester's eyes narrow, and his thin lips stretch across his face into a strange smile.

"Ha! Just delightful. Keep that sense of humor. It will serve you well. Yes, a perfect Christian replica. You won't be able to see it today."

"Because it would be catastrophic for the space-time continuum?"

Chris excitedly waits for Lester to react to his joke. Lester pauses, squints his eyes, and shakes his head.

"No, honestly, that makes no sense. You won't be able to see it today because it needs to be built. It's not magic, Christian."

"All right, never mind. I think you were about to tell me why we are doing this." Chris pushes the conversation, disappointed that Lester missed the classic science fiction reference.

"Moving forward, during some procedures, we will be giving you high doses of many drugs. I will do my best to control the dosing so that the effects will wear off before you need to be home, but some of your recovery times will extend beyond that, and it is possible that you may have an adverse reaction that extends past our schedule. In the event that you are unable to present yourself as you normally do, your highly convincing facsimile will be sent in your stead."

"Well, I guess he'll probably be better with Evelyn than I am anyway, right?" Chris jokingly smiles again and waits for Lester to follow suit.

"No, he will be exactly the same as you in every way. He will react to her in exactly the same fashion as you would."

"That poor kid is screwed."

Lester's head slightly tips to one side as the words visibly register in his expression. Slowly, his thin smile creeps onto his cheeks again. "Wait, that was meant to be humorous. Ha! Wonder-ful!"

.　　　.　　　.

Inside a white plastic tent within another white plastic tent in the center of Lester's personal workspace, Chris is lying naked and utterly alone on an operating table. Wires extend from circular patches on his head, chest, and every appendage of his body. IV tubes hang from each of his arms. His eyes squint to combat the in-tensity of the surgical light above him. The light blindingly reflects from every sterile white and silver surface surrounding him. He ima-gines this is what it would be like to be abducted by aliens. He's not entirely convinced that he hasn't been. His thoughts are interrupted by the button click of the intercom. Lester's voice comes through the speakers and bounces around the room.

Click. "Are you comfortable, Christian?" The button clicks again after Lester finishes his question.

"Ah, no! There's actually nothing comfortable about this at all." Chris is reluctant to express it aloud, but he isn't truly uncom-fortable in any way. His reaction is a self-trained response based on the emotion and experience of the person he once was, the person he was before Darkest Day.

Click. "I can adjust the temperature if you'd like?" *Click.*

"Yeah, I'm a little cold."

Click. "I see that." *Click.*

"Dude! Can we at least pretend you can't see my junk?"

Click. "I mean that I can see the temperature is below stand-ard room temperature by the readout, here, in the control room. I will raise the room temperature and administer something to make you more comfortable, but I cannot do too much as it may interfere with our results." *Click.*

"Oh, OK. Great."

The taste of rubbing alcohol collects in the back of Chris's throat. He is immediately warmer and more at ease than he'd already felt. This is the most relaxed he's been since Tom drugged him.

Click. "Just relax now, Chris." *Click.*

Stainless-steel walls hum as they rise alongside the operating table. Covered in metal robotic arms, computers, and various silver switches and buttons, the walls clunk and lock into place. Chris feels as though he is inside a high-tech, Swiss Army knife iron maiden. Padded posts rise out of the bed around his head and each of his joints. The posts tightly secure his entire body. Several steel rods with gray rubber balls on the ends slowly extend to Chris's face. The soft, smooth spheres press firmly into his skin.

The rods all shift slowly in and out of unison. As the rubber balls press and move against his skin, Chris's face contorts in every imaginable way.

Click. "Try to stay still and relax. Right now, we are mapping your expressions and the elasticity of your musculature. We will have to do this for every part of your body. We started with your face because this area is the most difficult, takes the longest, and we need to start somewhere, right? The next most difficult region is your genitals, but I thought we'd ease you into that." *Click.*

Chris's eyes widen. "Fantastic!" he garbles through his smashed lips.

·   ·   ·

Lester pens a note into his notebook as Chris buttons his shirt and ties his shoes. Chris is disheveled and still uncomfortable from the torture of the violating probes of his body mapping. He stands and openly adjusts his genitals. There is no reason to be shy at this point. After all, he just had every fold of skin on his penis inspected by a weird machine as Lester watched.

"So, do you know what caused everyone to be sterile? Was it the pesticides like the news and my asshole brother-in-law claim? Did we really do it to ourselves? Or was it somehow related to Darkest Day?" Chris tries to make casual conversation out of reflex.

Lester continues to write as he responds, "I can't say what it was exactly, but I can tell you that it wasn't the pesticides. That's not to say that they wouldn't have caused mass-sterility and killed us all eventually, but it would, however, have been much more miserably drawn out and much less comfortable."

"Are they really in everything?"

"For the most part, yes, but like everything else, it's much too late to do anything about it now." Lester's words drag without expression as he concentrates on his notes.

"Then why not program the mind control to stop people from thinking about it, so they don't have to feel guilty about how we poisoned ourselves or be angry about how our old government let it happen. Since there's nothing we can do about it, why allow people to worry about it at all?" Chris tries to peek over Lester's shoulder to read what he's writing.

Lester catches Chris prying. He drops his pen into the notebook and closes it defensively. Turning toward Chris, Lester is visibly annoyed at the distraction of Chris's questioning and his attempt to read the notes, "I couldn't take away all of our real problems. Without some hint of controversy or conspiracy and somewhere to direct our anger, no one would believe life was real with any amount of drugs. Distrust is so ingrained in us that we can't accept reality without it. People would be more suspicious if they had no reason to be suspicious. The truth is, everything designed by man to make life any different, or seem, or feel any different than what it actually is, has been killing us since we started making things to change the way life is or seems, or how it feels. We're done for today. There will be a car waiting for you when you arrive at work tomorrow. It's important that you physically walk into the building, just as you did today. Sensors in the area will recognize your presence and begin emitting a signal to your other coworkers arriving to work. This will allow you to walk to the car without anyone seeing you. Once the door closes behind you, you can turn around, walk back out, and get into the car. I'll see you then."

Chris is amused at the irony that Lester is bothered by having to speak with him after the wildly intrusive procedure and, well, absolutely everything else.

"What, no dinner after that?"

"My apologies, I don't have anything for you to eat." Lester's annoyance disappears. He is genuinely apologetic for not having something prepared for the event that Chris would be hungry.

Chris grins, amused once again by Lester's inability to sense his sarcasm.

"It was a jo... never mind. See you tomorrow."

19. Daddy's Little Drone

Chris's keys crash and scrape as they slide across the kitchen table. Cecilia quickly spins away from the kitchen sink.

"Chris, shh!" she whispers loudly, holding her finger against her lips. "I just got her down. I'm exhausted."

"Sorry," he freezes and whispers back.

He remains still as she picks up the monitor and stares with utter desperation at the screen.

"Okay, I think she's good."

Carefully, he places his bag onto the table while she walks by and kisses him.

"She's been fussy all day." She rechecks the monitor and sits down at the table. "So have I! I think the hormones are wearing off. I feel like I haven't slept in years. How was your day?"

"Totally normal."

The lie deflates him. As the words sigh out of his body, he pulls a can of beer out of the fridge and cracks it open. Cecilia's head whips toward him in wide-eyed terror at the loud noise. Chris freezes again with his hand still on top of the can. He grimaces and slowly pushes the tab back down to the top of the can. Cecilia holds her hand up with her index finger extended, signaling to him to cease all movement for a moment. She looks back at the monitor.

"There's no way she heard—"

Chris is interrupted by the lights flashing on the monitor. The baby must be making some sort of sound in the room. Chris can't hear it, but he knows by Cecilia's look of scornful disapproval that their fake baby is, in fact, crying.

"Damn it! She's up. You have to go in there. I absolutely cannot. I need to lie down for a while," she says, holding the monitor out to him.

Chris can't think of a single thing he wouldn't prefer to do than be trapped in that room with the drone, but this is not up for debate. Cecilia raises her eyebrows and shakes the blinking monitor at him. Anxiety grips his chest as he takes it. Cecilia walks into their bedroom and closes the door behind her. The monitor beeps as Chris turns it off and sips his beer. On the monitor screen, he can see the drone hovering over the bed in the nursery. Every muscle in Chris's neck tightens.

A thin band of red light followed by a quickly fading, red-light-grid circles the room. The grid scans over the features of every wall, the ceiling, the floor, and every object in the room, including Chris, as he steps into the nursery. Without taking his eyes off the drone hovering in the crib, Chris sits on the other side of the room in the plush rocking chair. Inside the crib, a pink blanket lies neatly folded around an infant onesie with a tiny matching knit cap above it. The whir of the propellers intensifies, and the drone rises just above the crib's rails. When it is a few inches over the rails, it stops moving, and the propellers quiet back to their regular volume. Red light extends from the robotic device as it spins clockwise, retracing the room. Chris squints at the light shining in his eyes as it crosses his expressionless face. He stares silently at the glowing light on top of the machine and drinks his beer.

He finishes his beer, sets the can on the changing table, and stands and crosses the room. His hand slowly extends to touch the drone, but it evades his finger and keeps itself just out of his reach. He tries again, but the device dodges his touch each time he reaches. The red-light scanner on the top of the machine circles with increasing speed until the grid appears continuous and constant on the entire nursery. Chris looks down. His entire body is hash-marked with the red light. Without looking back up at the drone, he suddenly reaches out with both hands to catch it. As it darts away from him, he nudges it with his grasping fingers, and it crashes into the wall. The red grid lines lose their axis and spin around the room. Three of the machine's propellers buzz violently with its body pinned to the wall by Chris's hands. Avoiding the propellers, he carefully grabs the device's body and pulls it toward him to inspect it.

He panics under his breath, "Fuck!"

The fourth propeller is motionless—possibly broken in the struggle, he thinks. He flicks at the still blade a few times, trying to get it to spin with the others. The broken blade doesn't respond. The laser grid tilts around the room with each movement.

"Son of a bitch!" he whispers to himself again.

The hallway light extends across the nursery from the opening door. Chris turns toward the door and hides the drone behind his back.

Cecilia groggily whispers through the crack, "Is everything okay in there? I heard a noise."

Chris whispers back, "Um, yeah, must've been outside. We're good. She's almost asleep. I'll be out soon, I think."

"K, I just wanted to check."

The thin band of light on the floor narrows and disappears as she silently closes the door.

Wind from revving propeller blades blows into Chris's face. He looks back down at the drone. With a plastic snapping sound, the drone's body pops open and startles Chris.

"Jesus Christ!"

His body revolts. He throws the device away from himself and jumps back away from it. It almost hits the floor before its functioning propellers can vary their speeds enough to keep the device hovering. Several precise needle-like mechanical arms reach out from the opening of the drone's separated body, and they begin to repair the broken blade. Smoke from a tiny soldering iron floats up from tiny metal arms as they prod around the damaged area. After a moment, the arms retract into the body, and it closes. The broken propeller whirs back to life and steadies the drone. It rises back to its previous position above the crib and restores the grid lines to a perfectly vertical and horizontal state. A band of red light from the top of the drone scans the room once more. As the light circles the room, the grid behind it vanishes. Chris squints again as the intense light flashes over his face and erases the grid from his skin. He backs away and slips out of the nursery.

20. Doughnuts and Other Visual Stimulations

"I had doughnuts on the table next to the door. Did you enjoy the doughnuts?"

Chris laughs and holds up a half-eaten glazed doughnut and a Styrofoam cup of coffee, "Yeah, Lester. The best part of my day so far. They're great, thank you."

"Again, allow me to apologize for being remiss in that I did not fully prepare for your needs on your last visit. I will have food available at all regular mealtimes moving forward."

"Excellent, Lester."

Lester smiles and pauses, satisfied with himself for righting his indiscretion.

"Wonderful. Finish up and let yourself into the OR. You can disrobe and get comfortable on the table. When you're ready, we will begin."

.   .   .

When Chris left the house this morning, he saw Tom and Julia with their drone toddler. He is still fuming about it while Lester connects him to the various nodes, tubes, and wires.

"I can't fucking believe that guy!"

"Who?" Lester responds while he continues his work, wiping the crook of Chris's arm with an alcohol pad.

"Tom. I always knew he was a total piece of shit, but to not tell his own sister she could have a kid! I mean, he knew the whole fucking time and just watched us struggle."

"This is something, from what I gather of Tom, that is completely within his character. Why would you be surprised?" Lester asks while he continues working.

"I don't know. I guess I'm not surprised. Of course, why wouldn't Tom hide a drone-baby from—ow! What the fuck?"

Lester looks up at Chris's pained, wincing face staring back at him.

"Oops, I missed the vein." Lester grabs Chris's arm, steadies it, and pulls the needle out while looking blankly at Chris.

"For the drone-baby comment? Seriously, Lester?" Chris asks.

"Perhaps." Lester returns his attention to Chris's arm.

"Dick," Chris whispers under his breath.

Looking back to Chris's arm, Lester reinserts the IV. Chris leans back against the headrest and continues to stare at the ceiling.

Lester continues the conversation, "Maybe you aren't upset with him, but rather at yourself. Tom is a liar, and you consider him to be unintelligent, yet you think he was able to fool you. However, you shouldn't allow it to affect you, though it is perfectly human to do so. It is also perfectly human to allow yourself to be misled. We would all like to think it impossible for ourselves to be convinced of a lie, but I assure you that it is not—not for any of us. You don't think less of Cecilia for not being able to see your child as you do. As a matter of fact, you prefer that she never does. Isn't that correct?" Lester's questioning is as pragmatic and unemotional.

"I guess not. Look, whatever. Honestly, I wish I didn't know any of this shit."

Lester pauses from tearing medical tape and looks Chris in the eyes. "Christian, if wishes and prayers were climbing the stairs, nothing would be at the top."

Chris's face distorts. "The fuck is that supposed to mean?"

"Nothing, I guess." Lester grins and shrugs his shoulder. He places tape and cotton over the IV injection. "I think you also may want to consider that maybe Tom doesn't know at all. Perhaps his wife kept it from him as well."

"Well, I guess that is possible. I mean, he is a fucking idiot." Chris pauses and cocks his head to the side. "Wait, you know he doesn't know. Christ, that's right! And you helped keep it from him by having Retsel give him a promotion and more work to do." He smiles, impressed with his own deductive reasoning.

"Tom couldn't be trusted. Measures had to be taken. Julia wasn't a typical candidate, but she found out through her job at the hospital, and after reviewing her case, an exception was made."

"You mean, when you found out how big of an asshole Tom was, you decided to let her have another kid so that she could be happy? Shit, you know everything! Who killed Kennedy?" Chris grins but honestly hopes Lester will tell him.

"Let's begin, shall we?" Lester pulls his notebook from his coat pocket and scribbles inside it, avoiding the question.

"Fine!" Chris flops his head back onto the headrest. "What are you writing in that thing all the time anyway?"

"Nothing of your concern, I assure you. Mostly notes on your treatment. You wouldn't comprehend it."

"I might understand!" Chris's face sours with defensiveness.

"Highly doubtful. I'm leaving now, and we will begin mapping with visual stimulation. You'll just need to relax and watch the screens. I have a headpiece specifically designed for you and this particular purpose. It does several things simultaneously, but this will still take several hours to complete. Just continue to watch the screen. If you need to release your bladder or bowels, simply do so. The bed will take care of it."

"Ew! Really? I think I'll hold it, thanks." The look on Chris's face switches from offended to disgusted.

"It's perfectly normal, Christian, but suit yourself. If you fall asleep, that's fine. We need to map both your conscious and unconscious brain. So, it won't make a difference. Also, be aware that when you fall asleep, and possibly while you're awake, you may experience intense visual, auditory, and olfactory hallucinations as I manually charge and deaden your synaptic connections."

He folds his notebook back together, slides it into his hip pocket, and retracts his pen tip with a click as he fastens the pen inside of his breast pocket.

The bed conforms to Chris's body and secures him as it tilts into a vertical position. Lester slides a white plastic helmet onto Chris's head.

"Awesome! Sounds like loads of fun." Chris tries to give a sarcastic thumbs-up, but the restraints limit him.

"Are you comfortable?" Lester asks.

"I feel like a major asshole with this giant white helmet."

"Well, it is an absolute achievement in brain mapping technology, but if you don't like the way it looks, by all means, let's use whatever you brought to do this," Lester mocks him.

"Take it easy, Dr. Smuggy. I was making a joke. Haven't you ever seen *Spaceballs*?"

"I'm afraid not." He holds a clear mouth guard up to Chris's face.

"Jesus! Why the hell do I need this? Are you going to electrocute me?"

"Don't be a baby, and yes, sort of. Trust me. You'll wish you'd worn it if you choose not to."

Chris allows him to place the rubber guard into his mouth.

As Lester leaves, the room goes dark, and a screen rises from the floor in front of Chris. The helmet's interior illuminates, casting a blue light on his face. A countdown image appears on the screen with a black number ten at the center, surrounded by two white concentric circles. The countdown begins with a line spinning clockwise. As the line sweeps behind the bold black numbers, the white screen inside the circle changes to gray. There is a beep in the headphones inside his helmet when the hand reaches twelve o'clock. Each time the hand makes a full rotation, there is another beep, and the number decreases by one while the circle behind the numbers turns from gray to white and back again. The sound of the beep is so stark in contrast to the still silence of the operating room that the volume is startling to him, even though he knows it's coming. Nine is gray. *Beep!* Eight is white. *Beep!* His heart races. Seven is gray. *Beep!* And so on.

"You can see the image, correct?" Lester's voice blasts into the helmet.

"Christ! Yes. Can you turn the volume down? It's loud as fuck in here." Chris mumbles through the mouth guard.

"Great. Sorry about the volume. Keep watching the screen." Lester's voice lowers inside the helmet, but it is still nearly deafening.

Nondescript, black and white shapes on gray backgrounds alternate with random, bold-colored images of a lighthouse on the ocean, a cat playing with yarn, and an impoverished child sitting in the dirt. Chris is void of any emotion for the images. He wonders if that's how he is supposed to feel. He doubts it.

The images play until he drifts off, but he doesn't know he's asleep. The screen and the beeping continue seamlessly in his dream, but he now recognizes the images. The taste of rubbing alcohol, which accompanied the other injections, flavors his breath again. These images are real, animate, and increasing in speed. They are distorted half-memories, and they begin to affect him—Kent's dead eyes from when Chris saw him in the warehouse, the blinking red light on the top of Evelyn, Tom's cartoon teeth laughing and scream-ing, Cecilia smiling at their wedding as Chris sings *The Sun Ain't Gonna Shine Anymore* into her ear. The background alters, they are high at the birthday party as they both continue to sing, and in be-tween each memory, the coffee stain on his cubicle wall sickeningly halts the motion of the dream for a moment. He sees his own, blue-lit face uncontrollably laughing and crying, but he somehow perceives the emotion separately from his body. Outside of himself, he can't feel the dread, terror, and joy he sees on his face. The feelings are not his own. He is a passive onlooker, unable to react. His body is help-less—fully surrendered to the pinned-down numbness of sleep paral-ysis.

To Chris, this is less like sleep and more like a waking nightmare-hallucination. The images flash in fast-forward. The beep-ing begins again—hundreds of marching soldiers in white hazmat suits with reflective black masks, *beep*, the dead stop of the coffee stain, *beep*, Evelyn's spinning propellers, *beep*, the still coffee stain, *beep*, from the day Decker told Chris about Building Blocks Labs, the face of the man from the bar fight as his features warp in slow motion with the impact of the large man's hand, *louder beep*, the cof-fee stain again, *excruciatingly loud beep*, Tyler waving his present around at the party, *drawn-out tone of an air horn and a distorted, crackling eardrum*. The coffee stain expands in front of him until it extends beyond his vision as he stands naked and dwarfed by its enormity—the revolting, overpowering stench of musty office, dust, and burned coffee grounds with a relentlessly blaring, flat-line-cacophony of a screaming heart monitor, all at the same time. His mind is reabsorbed into his body as the screeching continues. Drone propellers inside his body scrape through his flesh, ripping out of the skin on the underside of his wrists. The shrill tone peaks, muting the sound of his screams. He is pulled into the air by the whirring plastic propellers. Blood droplets spray onto his face and into his eyes and mouth from the spinning blades. He can feel the tendons in his shoulders and elbows tearing as he is lifted in front of the now infinitely stretching coffee-stained fabric wall. His blood leaches out of his body, draining upward and into the spinning blades. The wall is dyed red from the expanding blood spatters absorbing into the fabric.

His mouth waters, and his jaw reflexively clenches. Acid gurgles up his throat. He gags and coughs. Foamy vomit spills down his chest. Lester's hands in blue surgical gloves come into focus. He tips Chris's head forward, pulls the rubber guard out of his mouth, and wipes his face with a white towel.

"How are you feeling?"

Lester's voice is distorted, slow, and deep.

Chris tries to say something sarcastic. His mind forms the words, *fan-fucking-tastic, wonderful*, but he is unable to force his mouth to articulate them with his cramping jaw. A moan escapes his throat. While Lester fidgets with the helmet, the sweat on Chris's brow cools in the breeze of Lester's breath. The pounding in Chris's chest slows. His entire body weakens. His vision blurs and fades, surrendering to sleep.

.　　.　　.

The scratching of a fine point pen against the textured paper of Lester's notebook wakes Chris. Lester sits nearby in a white leather recliner, writing something in his book on his lap.

"How are you feeling now?" Lester asks without looking up from his notes.

"Good, actually! Refreshed, like I've had an amazing full night of sleep." Chris realizes this, to his astonishment, mid-sentence.

"You have. Thirty full days and nights of sleep, to be exact."

Chris jumps and sits up.

"Are you fucking serious? I've been in this bed for a whole fucking month!"

Lester closes his notebook and meets Chris's anxious stare. "Yes, but there's no need to worry. You have not been missed."

Chris reels, "Well, that's just fucking great, isn't it?"

Lester's head shakes in a patronizing manner. "Of course, that's not what I meant. I meant that every detail was taken into account, electrical stimulation for your musculature, complete nutrients through IV, you won't be any worse for wear. You're better than normal. You said it yourself. Your android effectively handled your presence at home and with your friends. Remember? He's like you in every way. Everything was done in the exact way in which you would have handled it, and, to all appearances, it was, in fact, you who handled it. Cecilia is none the wiser."

Chris relaxes back down onto the bed. "Well, if you say so." In utter exasperation, he raises his arms and allows them to flop back onto the bed at his sides.

"See for yourself."

Chris looks over to Lester, who points in the direction of a perfect replication of Chris standing on the other side of the room. Chris sits back up and swings his legs off the bed. He is equally enamored and disturbed by his doppelganger. Holding together the back of a hospital gown he does not recall putting on, he walks over to the visibly perfect copy of himself.

Lester stands and joins Chris next to the android.

"Impeccable, isn't it?"

"It's fucking freaky!" Chris whispers.

"We have been remotely downloading his entire sensory program and uploading his full experience into your mind using several electrodes, which I took the liberty of attaching to you. I assumed you would not want to miss anything. In a few moments, you'll remember everything that happened to your android in the past thirty days as if they were your own memories. They will come all at once, though. You may want to sit down. It can be quite disorienting."

"I'm good." Chris ignores Lester and continues to study his replica.

"Suit yourself. It is magnificent, isn't it?" Lester smiles in the reverie of his creation.

Unconsciously, Chris reaches out to touch the scar on its bottom lip. With his other hand, he feels the lump of scar tissue on his own bottom lip. He's had the lump since he split his lip on a coffee table when he was seven. His finger runs over the hard tissue, and a wave of mundane daily occurrences floods his perception. In staggering fast-forward, he recalls everything—eating dinner, putting the drone to bed, the darkness of sleep, waking, breakfast, giving the drone a bottle, a kiss goodbye from Cecilia, kissing the drone goodbye, driving to work, assembling drones at work, having drinks with Decker, driving home, kissing the drone's nonexistent projection, kissing Cecilia, having dinner, sitting in the dark nursery, staring at the red light of the drone, and the darkness of sleep. The process repeats thirty times at a nauseating speed. The rapid, flashing visions dizzy him. He loses his balance but clutches the shoulder of his robotic twin to steady himself.

"Oh! Chris, you look quite pale. You should sit back down." Lester takes him by the wrist and places a hand on his back to guide him back to the bed. "I'm sure this is all quite a bit to take after the drugs and neural stimulation. Rest for a while, and then let yourself out. Your clothes are on the humanoid. Go home, and I'll prepare the next steps. I'll send a drone for you when everything here is ready for us to continue."

21. Home Is Where the Drone Is

Lying awake in bed next to Cecilia, all Chris can focus on is the static buzzing of drone propellers coming from the baby monitor. Cecilia has been asleep for hours. He rolls onto his side, wrapping his pillow around his head and over his ears to muffle the noise. His arms squeeze the pillow more tightly against his head, but the sound is still there. He lets go of the pillow and turns the alarm clock to see the time. It's five AM, an hour before the alarm typically goes off to wake him for work. Cecilia moans and rolls toward him. He slides the button on the alarm to the off position.

Cecilia's voice is groggy. "Everything okay, hon?"

"Yeah, I just wanted to get to work early today. Sorry, I didn't mean to wake you," he whispers back to her.

She yawns, "Okay, can you check on Evie before you get ready? Just make sure she's breathing. I know it's dumb."

"It's not dumb," he responds.

It's not dumb because, from what he's been told, every parent does this, but also because Evelyn is not breathing. *"She never has, and she never will,"* he thinks as he reaches to pet Cecilia's head. "I'll check in on her."

She rolls away from him. Chris quietly stands and walks to

the door.

"Oh"—she stops him as he turns the door handle—"and that list of stuff I needed you to pick up three days ago is still on the fridge. Can you try not to forget it today?"

"Three days?" he wonders. He's only been home for two days. Admittedly, he did forget that she asked him to do it yesterday, but she must've been talking to android Chris the first time she asked. Maybe the robot was made too well. It forgot the same shit he did.

"I won't forget." As he says it, he remembers saying it yesterday too. He also remembers the robot's memory of saying the same thing when she first asked. The process of recalling the robot's memory is not seamless, but this is precisely how it would have worked, even if it had been him instead of the robot the first time she asked. "Incredible," he accidentally whispers aloud as he closes the door.

The baby doesn't need to be checked. He knows it doesn't, but Cecilia might be watching on the monitor, so he's forced to at least walk into the room and stand over the crib for a moment. He takes a deep breath and opens the door to the nursery. The drone scans him as he enters. Looking down into the bed, he tries to imagine what his child would actually look like, but he can only picture the blurred television static from the pictures Cecilia made him take to work with him.

The eerily familiar click of Lester's surgery room intercom stops Chris's heart and pulls his attention up to the baby monitor camera. He half-expects Lester's voice to come through its speakers.

Cecilia whispers through the monitor, "Thank you." *Click.*

Chris waves to the camera and leaves the room.

•   •   •

Kent's tiny, orange smart car is the only other car in the O.K. Package parking lot. Chris is more than an hour early. There isn't a drone waiting for Chris in the lobby. He reluctantly presses the up button for the elevator, and the doors open immediately. The car rises smoothly to the seventh floor. No one is there. He didn't expect anyone to be there, but it makes him feel lonelier somehow. He walks past Kent's, his, and Decker's empty desks to the break room. The mechanical wheels inside the money slot on the vending machine whine and slowly tug the dollar bill out of Chris's hand. He presses a button, and a can of soda clunks to the bottom.

Even Paula's eardrum-destroying excuse for a voice would be welcomed over the oppressive quiet of the office. Chris shuffles down the stairs to the warehouse catwalk door. The faint, unmistakable timbre of Kent's falsetto singing voice bleeds into the stairwell.

"Kent!" Chris shouts, opening the door.

"Hey, Kent!" He shouts again as he grabs the railing to bend over it and look down into the warehouse.

"Hey, Kent." His voice lowers, defeated by the realization that Kent will not be any sort of company. "Nice to see a little mind control doesn't stop you from kissing all that ass."

Chris sits down on the catwalk with his feet dangling. His elbows rest on the lowest rung of the railing, his chin on the next. The tab of his soda cracks under his hand. Soda foam sprays and drips down onto the warehouse floor. He sips from the can and watches Kent tape and stack boxes. Kent's headphones are in his ears, and he sings at the top of his lungs. Still, Chris can tell from the lifeless movements of Kent's body and the listless look on his face that even if the weird little man weren't listening and screaming along to Belinda Carlisle, he still wouldn't hear Chris calling him.

Kent's cracking, toneless voice fills the warehouse with incorrect lyrics.

"Ooh, don't you know what it's..."

Skrawk! The tape gun censors his vocals.

"I'll tell you, Heaven..."

Thump... Skrawk! He drops the box to the floor and tapes another.

"Called Earth..."

Chris swings his legs and nods his head to the beat of the song.

A drone flies into the warehouse from the hallway leading to the lobby. Over Kent's singing, Chris can hear Lester's voice calling to him from the drone.

"Here we go." Chris gulps the rest of his soda and climbs down the stairs to meet the drone.

As Chris approaches, Lester's voice comes out of the drone again. "We're ready for you now."

The drone turns back to the hall. Chris follows it out of the warehouse.

22. Inappropriate Questions

Looking directly at the ceiling of the white tent, the white edges of the electrode riddled helmet act as peripheral blinders, and he can only see one infinite dimension of perfect, colorless, uninhabited space. It feels as if the stark, white emptiness is pressed flush against his eyes. It is all that exists, and it is as terrifying as absolute darkness. He turns his head to see the stainless-steel equipment. The gauges and robotic arms prove that the hollow nothingness is a mirage. Seeing something—anything other than blank white allows him to feel as though he is a part of reality again.

Ambient beeps and white noise follow the amplified click of the talk button on the control room microphone. Lester's voice, in full stereo surround, fills the tent.

Click. "We're going to try some auditory stimuli. Please listen to my questions and think about how you would naturally respond. I switched back to the intercom. You were right. The audio in the helmet is malfunctioning for some strange reason." *Click.*

"You mean in the absolute achievement in brain mapping technology helmet, helmet?"

Click. "Yes, the very same." *Click.* Lester is not amused.

"Sounds good."

Click. Faint cackling comes over the intercom.

"I get it." Lester's voice cracks. "Auditory stimuli... sounds good." He continues to laugh and catch his breath. "You really are a crack-up, Christian." *Click.*

"OK, yeah, that one wasn't supposed to be a joke," Chris responds into the white void above him.

Click. "Happy accident, then, I guess." Lester's voice quickly straightens, "Let's get right to it, shall we? How do you feel about Tom?" *Click.*

"Honestly, I hate that fucking guy, but there is something about hating him that makes me more comfortable in my own skin. Once in a while, he surprises me, but—" the click of the intercom interrupts Chris.

Click. "While I honestly do find what you're saying quite interesting and considerably, what you would refer to as 'messed-up,' I only need you to think about how you would respond. I don't need you to say it aloud. Do you understand?" *Click.*

"Got it."

Click. "Wonderful. Think of how you would describe your feelings toward Cecilia. Just think, don't say." *Click.*

Chris lies in still silence, thinking about Cecilia when he told her they might be able to have a child. He pictures her nervously smiling face with tears welling in her eyes.

Click "Perfect. Now, do you prefer to masturbate while you're seated or while you're standing?" *Click.*

"What?" Chris's expression twists. He tries to turn his head to look into the camera.

Click. Lester sighs into the microphone. "This isn't Simon Says, Christian. I'm not trying to trick you into talking. Please, keep your thoughts internalized. I cannot get an accurate reading with you shouting at every question." *Click.*

"Well, why would you even ask me that?" Chris shouts.

Click. "I'm trying to evoke your response to being offended, which is clearly sensitive, but I don't have an accurate reading, so we'll have to move on to alternate and more engaging stimuli. It is important that you do not respond. Emotions tend to become more intense the longer we wait to express them. Apart from that, I think you should know that masturbation is a perfectly normal and healthy practice for humans and many other species. Now, may we proceed?" *Click.*

"Sure, sorry. Go ahead."

Click. "What is your earliest memory?" *Click.*

Chris tries to remember, but nothing comes. He stares at the blank whiteness of the tent ceiling and thinks of Tom's cartoon teeth laughing on the front lawn, Cecilia with the empty blanket in her arms as she looked at him from her hospital bed, and the red grid laser light of the drone scanning his face.

Click. "Wait, do you not enjoy masturbating, Christian?" *Click.*

Chris grits his teeth and rolls his eyes, breathing loudly through his nose and thinking about his answer while awaiting the next irritating question.

The intercom clicks again, allowing Lester's voice through as he laughs, "Oh, right! Sorry, Christian. You can answer that. That was a question I was asking out of my own curiosity." *Click.*

Chris tries to turn his head to the camera again, but his face just mashes awkwardly against the inside of the helmet. He shouts, "Are you fucking serious, Lester? Let's just get back to the stupid test!"

Click. "Okay, okay! I guess we can check off predisposition toward hostility in the mid to high range." *Click.*

Chris angrily jolts against the restraints.

Click. "How does it feel to know that you will die?" *Click.*

.   .   .

"We're ready for the surgery to repair the synapses," Lester says as he comes into the observation tent where Chris is finishing getting dressed. Lester taps a few times on the keyboard of a laptop he holds open in his arm. "I decided the best course of action will be to implant receivers and transmitters, which will filter the information as it enters your perception. You should be left with only the information necessary to experience the reality to which you were previously accustomed. It should be a short procedure with minimal recovery time. The incisions will be microscopic." He closes the laptop, sits down at his desk, and pulls the notebook out of his lab coat pocket. He begins to write while he continues speaking. "We can do it first thing tomorrow and probably have you back to your previous routine within three weeks. There will be no visible scarring or pain from the surgery. When you wake up, you will be completely healed. It'll be as if nothing has happened, except that your life will look a lot more like it did before, and you'll perceive Evelyn and all the other Stereopticons as children."

Lester turns to Chris and waits for a response.

"Sweet! I can't wait."

"Perfect." Lester returns his attention to his notebook and addresses Chris without looking at him. "Christian, can I ask you another question, apart from the treatment?"

"Sure, I guess."

His head remains lowered, and he continues to write into the leather notebook. "It's one I asked you already."

"Just ask, Lester."

"The question was, how does it feel to know that you would die? How would you answer it if you were to say it aloud?" His head stays buried in his book.

Chris rubs his hands together for a moment, unable to think of a response. "I guess I don't know."

Lester laughs as he looks up at Chris. "That's so funny. That's how they all answer it. Well, we'll see you tomorrow." His head points back down to what he is writing.

"Wait... all? You mean other people have gone through this?"

Lester stops writing, slides his pen into his chest pocket, and focuses on Chris again. "Yes, of course! Several others have had these procedures. How did you think all of this was so readily available to you?" He holds his page with a finger as he gestures around the open warehouse and the medical tent. "Did you think you were the only one?"

"Well, yeah, I guess, kind of." Looking down sheepishly, he feels stupid for assuming he was the only person to ever be in this situation.

"Don't be embarrassed. That's also what everyone thinks. Allow me to ask you this, do you believe yourself to be unique?"

Chris looks back up, more confident in his words. "No, no, not really."

Lester's head twists like a dog's does when hearing a new sound. His face looks pleasantly surprised. "Really? Huh! None of the others said that." His eyes trail away from Chris into the ether for a second. "Huh."

"What happened to the others? Are there people out there who know all of this?"

"No one who lives a public life. Some we caught early and were able to treat under the guise of psychiatric therapy. They believed they had hallucinated something weird at work or a drone here or there. We were able to adjust these glitches easily with medication to alter their physiological response to the broadcast suggestions and the other drugs now present in our atmosphere. Others, unfortunately, completely lost their minds and were unable to function in society. I assure you, those who fall into that category were much less sound of mind than you are currently, well before any of this was an issue for them. A few opted for electroconvulsive therapy. While removing their memories was almost entirely successful in every case, the degree to which they were able to return to their regular lives varied greatly. It's quite barbaric. We changed the company policy just before you and I met. We no longer offer this as an option. Only the Beta Sciences twelve-member board, including myself, understands the full scope of our actual reality."

The chair and Lester's face spin back toward the desk. Chris slides his blazer over his white button-down shirt. From across the room, he can hear Lester's pen click and begin to scribble.

"See you tomorrow." Chris thumbs his bag onto his shoulder.

Lester waves with the back of his hand without turning around.

Chris walks through the city block length warehouse toward the exit with the sounds of Lester writing at a furious pace behind him. He glances back as he opens the door. Lester flips the page and continues to write without pause.

23. Surgery and Recovery

Chris wasn't nervous about the surgery until this moment as he walks into the surgical tent and finds four Lesters prepping for the procedure. The Lesters ignore him as they go about their business of checking monitors and equipment and adjusting a monstrosity of silver arms connected to a halo over the table Chris has now been strapped to more times than he'd like to remember. The stainless-steel arms look exactly like the ones that came out of Evie when it was repairing itself, but there are thousands of them. They extend a few feet from the skull-sized halo and bend back to the center. The steel arms bend again at a second joint over the halo and point down toward the center. They remind him of the stiff shriveling legs of a dead spider or the framework of a carnival ride made of dental tools. Knowing that his head will be in the center of it in moments, he stares at the mess of metal appendages with every writhing inch of his guts begging him to turn around and walk out. Chris thinks to himself that he should have woken up Cecilia to tell her he loved her, he should have checked to make sure his last will and testament were updated, he should have apologized to Tom again, been nicer to Kent. His thoughts scold him for being so neglectful.

"Christian." The voice of a fifth Lester calls from behind Chris.

"Jesus Christ! Lester, you scared the shit out of me!" The tic of Chris's gown comes loose as he jumps. His hands scurry to collect the flapping fabric of his gown together in the back.

"Don't be skittish. It is perfectly human and natural to be fearful, but there's a very low probability of you dying," Lester reassures him.

"Oh! I feel better now. Thank you." Chris's sarcasm couldn't be more obvious, but, once again, it is wholly lost on Lester.

"Oh, you're welcome, friend." Lester smiles. "I see you've met Lester Two, Three, Four, and I believe you met Five on the car ride to your first visit. Say hello to Christian, everyone."

"Hello, Christian." The exact recreations turn and welcome Chris in a chorus of four cringe-inspiring Lester voices.

"Hey, Lesters." He gives them an uncomfortable wave and leans to whisper to Lester One, who he assumes is the true Lester. "This is all pretty fucking creepy, Lester."

"Everything is fine, Christian. The other Lesters are only here to get everything in place. Thank you, Lesters." The other Lesters follow each other in numerical order out of the room.

"And what the fuck is that thing?" Chris points at the nightmare contraption of metal spider legs.

"Oh, this?" Lester circles around the machine with his hand running over its thousands of arms. "This is the most sophisticated brain surgery equipment ever created. Trust me. You would not want my fallible human hands performing these delicate procedures. This magnificent device far surpasses our needs today. Believe me when I say you are in good hands. I engineered and programmed this myself, well, with the assistance of my several other selves."

Lester playfully pats the bed under the machine.

"Come, lie down. This will be over before you realize."

Chris timidly lies on the bed. He looks up through the middle of a halo created by the needle-pointed tips of the thousands of robotic arms.

"Fuck it! Do your worst, Lester."

Lester comes into view between Chris's face and the machine.

"That's the spirit." Lester places a clear rubber mask over Chris's mouth and nose. "Now, just breathe normally."

The circle of white light shining down through the machine dims into Chris's euphoric darkness.

.   .   .

Light pierces through Chris's eyelids, waking him. His body is anchored with suffocating paralysis. Panic swells his chest. He can only look directly ahead into the light between the pulsating arms of the machine, scraping and grating against one another. The AM radio-tuning-metallic-screech of the colliding components is deafening as he is pushed toward the light into a lengthening tunnel of reticulating steel tentacles. He fights with his dead muscles to move. The light vanishes, and the cold metal tears into his flesh. Everything disappears into colorless darkness, freeing his body. He jerks awake, gasping for air.

The surgery is over, as is the nightmare. This is recovery. Aside from the fading terror that woke him, he feels amazing, rested, and excited. An involuntary stretch contorts his entire body. He happily grunts and moans while his body slides around between the sheets. His legs swing off the side of the bed, and he sits up.

"Lester!" Chris turns and calls out in the direction of the medical tent and control room.

There's no response. Behind Lester's desk, his lab coat hangs over the back of his chair. From the bed, Chris can see Lester's notebook and pen peeking out of the hip pocket of the coat. Chris surveys the room once more. There is no sign of Lester—no sign of any of the Lesters. He hops off the bed onto the cold cement floor covered in imaginary needles and broken glass.

"Ah! Fuck!"

Chris's legs crumble under his weight. His body drops to the floor in a pile on top of his numb, tingling feet. He slowly pulls himself up using the bed and the recliner next to it, and he steps cautiously toward the desk. The prickly blood returns to his lower extremities with each step. Millions of tiny bee stings punish him as he slowly makes his way to Lester's desk. The stinging moves up to his butt and the backs of his bare legs when they hit the seat. Rolling the chair toward the desk, he pulls the notebook from the coat's pocket. As he places it on the desk, the book opens where Lester's pen holds a place between the most recently filled page.

Surgical Procedures

Subject 428 Adams, Christian

Frontal Lobe

-enhance broadcast suggestion receptivity

-micro drill incision

-implant: Thermoelectric Low Voltage Stimulator

Temporal Lobe

-divert focus of selective auditory stimuli to include frequency masking broadcast signals

-laser incision

-implant: Beta Electro Sensory Receiver

Parietal Lobe

-override sensory processing

-modify perception of projected imagery

-micro drill incision

-implants: ESR and Neutral Ground Dampener

Occipital Lobe

-distort primary visual cortex to emphasize frequency masking broadcast signals over underlying objects

-additional filtration of information entering ventral stream

-laser incision

-implant: Beta Data Biochip Receiver and Transmitter, Beta Neuron Filter

His fingers search his scalp for the healing incisions, but there is nothing. He turns the page and continues to read.

Recovery

Subject 428 Adams, Christian

Day 1:

-laser cauterized incisions healing as expected

-all ESRs functioning at 100%

-minor damage to Parietal Lobe caused an increase in sexual stimulation, expecting a full recovery and return to normal as the swelling decreases

-continued anesthesia

Day 2:

-incisions healing at or above projected speeds

-ESRs re

-overall brain swelling decreased by 30%

-no decrease in ancillary swelling - subject continues to "pitch a tent"

"Lester, you perv!" Chris stops reading and reaches under his robe to check on his '*increased sexual stimulation.*' "Well, the swelling appears to have subsided," he says aloud and chuckles to himself.

Returning his attention to the book, he thumbs through to earlier pages. Most pages are covered in equations that look more like hieroglyphics to Chris. Other pages are sketches of the giant hovering filtration airships and flying wind turbines. He remembers them filling the skies during the months after Darkest Day. He stops on another page with a drawing of a rocket. This drawing, he recognizes from several places, multiple news stories of the Beta Sciences launches during the cleanup after Darkest Day, but more immediately from the crude representations of the rockets used for Darkest Day fireworks and countless other ornaments and souvenirs that fill every store for months before every Darkest Day celebration. "Our darkest days behind us, our brightest ahead" is the slogan playfully written on every item and said countless times by everyone during the annual celebrations. The real rockets, which also bared the encouraging catchphrase, were utilized to create mid-air explosions and divert fallout and pollutants to less populated regions. They also dispersed chemicals to counteract the effects of the toxins and radiation. Earth-shaking explosions went on for days. At the time, no one had any idea that it was Beta Sciences. No one had any clue what it was at all. They just assumed they were all going to die very soon.

Chris can remember duct-taping plastic over the windows at the house with Cecilia and thinking it was absurdly pointless, but that was what they remembered seeing in all the movies depicting end-of-the-world nuclear fallout. Later, Retsel would do several radio shows, internet streams, and television broadcasts to explain it all. Now that Chris knows more about the explosions than he ever wanted to, he can't help laughing to himself—Retsel was everyone's hero, and he isn't even human. He did nothing. Very little is more satisfying to Chris than thinking of Tom's bullshit stories about meeting Retsel now that Chris knows Retsel isn't any more real than Tom's front teeth.

The sketched diagram of the rocket is exquisitely detailed. Chris is blown away by Lester's artistic abilities. He isn't sure whether he should be happy or disappointed that Lester didn't include a drawing of Chris's *"ancillary swelling."* Maybe that's on another page. He laughs again, considering the possibility.

There are several drawings of each separate part of the rocket. Every component is separately described in explicit detail on the following pages—*Propulsion System, Guidance System Elements, Engine, Warhead Payload.*

He reads the sub-heading under *Warhead Payload* aloud, "*Atmospheric Sterilization and Radiated Material Additives: Initial Stage.* What in the fuck?"

His finger traces down the list on the page.

Hexachlorocyclohexane (endocrine disruption)

Polychlorinated Biphenyl (modified irradiated dicamba, glyphosate) Dichlorodiphenyltrichloroethane

Tetrachloroethylene

Cyclophosphamide

Actinomycin D

Alternate with Potassium Iodide dispersions.

Reading through the list, he can feel his chest filling with a familiar, pained throbbing of horror and panic. Aside from Potassium Iodide, which he also recalls from the news stories and old movies because it was used to combat the effects of radiation, all the chemicals on the list are the same chemicals that every fertility doctor mentioned when telling Cecilia and him about all the possible reasons for everyone becoming sterile. *This doesn't make any sense*, he thinks. *Lester couldn't have released these into the atmosphere for any other reason.*

Chris jumps out of the chair, tearing off his gown.

"Lester!" he shouts while he sloppily dresses. With Lester's notebook hanging from his teeth, he quickly pulls up and buttons his pants. He struggles to get his shoes on his feet while running out of the room.

He shouts louder. "Lester! Fuck!" His shoe slips onto his foot, and he falls to the ground in the doorway. Running out into the warehouse, he shouts again, "Lester!" His voice echoes through the room.

Retsel steps out of the control room next to the white tent.

"Oh, great! You're awake."

Retsel's mouth moves, but it's Lester's voice and Lester's words that come out. Lester's voice isn't only coming from Retsel's mouth, it's being played at a mind-numbing volume through the audio system all around the warehouse.

Retsel is irritatingly dashing. His hair is as perfectly sculpted as his jawline. The blue suit he's wearing is pressed to perfection and is a flawless fit. Regardless of what Chris now knows, he still has an instinctual reverence for Retsel. Chris tugs at his own shirt to adjust it. Annoyed with himself for feeling the need to correct his disheveled appearance and being unable to keep himself from doing so, he fixes his collar and buttons his shirt as he approaches Retsel. He glares at Retsel's face. With the knowledge of what Retsel is, there is something newly grotesque and artificial about his appearance.

Lester's voice barks over the sound system again. Retsel's mouth continues to move along with Lester's words.

"I thought it might be easier for you to have someone around when you woke. The surgery was a complete success, so you can no longer see me by traditional methods. You can only hear me because I'm broadcasting my voice on Retsel's frequency. I'm still here, but only virtually. I'm seeing and hearing you through Retsel's perception feed."

The typically grading pitch of Lester's voice is intensified exponentially with the added volume and echo of the sound system.

"Well, Christ! Can you turn the volume down? You sound like a goddamn fire drill. It's worse than the helmet was."

"Oops, sorry," Lester's voice cuts from the speakers. "I accidentally had Retsel's Bluetooth connected. Pardon my faux pas." His voice is quieted and begins to only come from Retsel's mouth. Retsel's body and face act out a resounding belly laugh, but only Lester's silly little cackle is produced.

"What the fuck is this, Lester? Chris shakes the notebook at Retsel, holding it open to the page with the description of the sterilization chemicals. He holds it as close as he can to Retsel's face without touching him. "What in the fuck is this?"

Retsel's face turns away from the pages being waved accusingly in his face. Chris lowers the book and stares at Retsel, waiting for an answer. Retsel turns back, snatches the notebook from Chris's hand, and scolds him with a stern look of disapproval. This is Lester's look of irritation, but it is somehow perfectly transplanted onto Retsel's features.

"This is mine, and it was not meant for your eyes. Your invasion of my privacy shows a severe lack of judgment and trust on your part, but to answer your question, it is a note in one of my personal journals. It describes the first chemical components released during atmospheric filtration for the initial phase of the post-Darkest Day air purification process."

"Trust! Invasion of your privacy! You've got to be fucking joking, right? Why in the hell is it made of every single chemical that every fertility doctor has ever warned Cecilia and me about? You're a fucking genius, right? So, don't tell me you don't know all of this shit causes sterility. Some are radioactive drugs used for cancer patients, for Christ's sake. You were fucking poisoning all of us. Darkest Day isn't the reason no one can have kids. You are! And just so you know, it's actually pretty fucking hard to talk to you and look at this fucking guy!" Chris points at Retsel. "For the record, this is not better. This is fucking creepy as shit!"

Lester scoffs, "Well, I apologize for trying to make you comfortable, Christian, but poisoned? Really? The chemicals I released have not been responsible for a single recent death. Most of them are responsible for saving millions of lives. Most of them were farmed from what already existed in our atmosphere, soil, and water supplies."

"Oh, well, in that case, Lester, let me be the first to say how happy I am that you at least recycled the human race ending chemicals. And here I was, thinking that you were being neglectful!"

Lester's voice calms, "Look." Retsel's body steps and turns to stand next to Chris. "Allow me to explain everything."

The android reaches out and places its hand on Chris's back to calm him and lead him to sit down at a stainless-steel table. Chris flinches from Retsel and pushes the robotic hand off his back but takes a seat at the table anyway. Retsel takes the seat across from him.

"You see, tragedy always interested me--how it affects us, how we grow from it, not only emotionally but physiologically as well. When I was much younger, I began to study the residual effects on the human condition due to mass genocide or large-scale loss of life due to disease or anything of that nature."

"Sounds like an awesome fucking childhood." Chris does nothing to hide the disturbed and disgusted look on his face.

"Oh, it was!" Retsel's face, commanded by Lester's movements, momentarily looks up and away from the conversation as he reminisces. "At any rate, after years of research, founding Beta Sciences, and devoting all my faculties to better understanding the aftermath of widespread death. My research immediately after Darkest Day led to a conclusion that would not be popular with the general public. Still, a small consortium of brilliant scientific minds from the board of Beta Sciences who had been privy to the research all drew the same conclusion I had. As outlandish as it may have sounded, the research was conclusive. The collective consciousness is derived from a single, solitary soul."

"Soul? Really, Lester? Doesn't sound very fucking sciencey!" Chris's tone is sharp and biting.

"The existence of a soul and a true beginning was the last great unproven science. Religion is merely an unproven theory, like any other hypothesis. All factual matters of science were, at one time, beliefs or guesses. After Darkest Day, our theory was measurable in real-time. The existence of the soul is no longer a theory or a belief. The research was conclusive. You don't have to call it that if it makes you uncomfortable. It took me some time to wrap the emo-

176

tional part of my brain around the term."

Rubbing the back of his neck, Chris struggles to understand. "I still don't follow you. So, we have souls, not exactly a revelation. You could have learned all about it at Sunday school. Get to the part where you take away the ability of every fucking living person to create life!"

"Well, actually, it was quite a revelation, indeed. I'm not talking about belief structures or religion. I'm talking about measurable scientific evidence of a completely new understanding of existence and how we came to be. And I didn't say, souls. I said, soul, singular." Retsel holds up one finger in defiance and correction.

"Okay! Soul! Whatever! Get on with it!" Chris smacks the robot's hand down and waves his own in the air to signal that the conversation is in drastic need of being expedited.

Once again, Lester's expression of irritation ghoulishly takes form on Retsel's face. "When considering our human history, the statistics showed society always had an uptick in emotional well-being directly following a great war or catastrophic loss of life. That is to say, those who weren't directly affected by the casualties showed greater signs of self-actualization, artistry, intellect, et cetera. Armed with only that knowledge, the change in the general intellect of society might easily be attributed to the way a shared traumatic experience binds and inspires groups of people or possibly the effect of camaraderie shared by those with a common goal or enemy. What I'm telling you is the actual reason. It may not approach something you would allow yourself to consider to be the meaning of life, but this is the reason for it, and that reason is simple, run-of-the-mill loneliness."

"Lester, what the fuck are you talking about?"

"At the knowable beginning of existence, which is to say, from the moment a soul or consciousness existed, there was a single mind, a solitary soul or conscience. This is decided, and I assure you, accurate. My only guess, albeit a highly educated guess, as to the reason for what happened next was out of the desire for companionship. This original soul divided itself. Subsequently, those souls divided themselves, and so on, until we are here, now. After Darkest Day, we understood that the reason for the uptick was the redistribution of the soul back into the remaining living. Interestingly enough, without Darkest Day, we may have never discovered any of this. The redistribution of the soul was, without question, the cause of our newly found levity and ability to understand. With this new understanding of our existence, the greatest minds of our time, myself and the Board of Beta Sciences, decided we would make it our goal to allow one human to experience the complete reunification of that original soul."

Lester's complacent tone is only more confounding to Chris.

"Oh, I get it. You're fucking crazy! Your plan is to let us all die until there is only one of us?"

"Not exactly. What we did was ensure that no additional lives would be created until the soul could be complete again," with Retsel's mouth, Lester corrects Chris.

"Why save the world at all if what you really wanted was for everyone to die? It doesn't make any goddamn sense!" Chris shouts out of astonishment and frustration. "Why not let the radiation and riots kill us all? It would have been a lot quicker."

Lester's shock at the suggestion flashes on Retsel's face. "You can't honestly be asking me this question. That would hardly be the act of a decent, enlightened person. I find it highly uncivilized to allow people to suffer. I'm not a monster, Christian! Do you think I'm a monster?"

"Fuck yes, I think you're a monster! Look at you right fucking now! What the fuck would you call it?" Chris yells.

Retsel's face looks mildly offended. He pauses to glance down at the rest of his body and back up to continue the conversation.

"A monster would cause suffering or allow it to continue, at the very least. I saved everyone from horrific fates of agonizing, torturous deaths. Don't you understand everyone would have suffered without my help, and eventually, at some point, we would have all died anyway? What we are talking about isn't truly death at all. We are talking about putting ourself back together," Lester/Retsel explains with Lester's typical cadence and control.

"Let's say any of this is right. Don't you think the soul will be lonely again once everyone is gone? If you're right, and this is how life came to be, don't you think it'll just divide itself again? Then won't this all be for nothing?" Chris tries to reason with the robot and Lester.

"An incredibly insightful question, but even humans, before the idea of reconstituting the divided soul, had evolved past the need for authentic interactions with one another. Preventative and calculated measures are being taken, I assure you."

Lester's voice remains calm while Chris grows increasingly aggravated.

"Do you think you're God already? You took our free will and decided our entire fate based on what really just boils down to your own fucking opinion! People can't decide what they want if they don't know what they should be allowed to know. And what if you're wrong? What if the only reason people have the emotional well-being uptick, or whatever the hell you called it, is because, after all that death and destruction, people just value life more?"

"Once again, I assure you, this is not an opinion and certainly does not belong to me alone. Besides, what does it matter if what we truly were, was nothing? We were billions of seemingly insignificant bits of an archaic thing from the beginning of time. That perfectly whole, primeval entity was divided again and again until it became the inconceivably loathsome, empty, and unrecognizable us. We are infinitesimal, separately meaningless fragments of that which came before us—inconsequential parts of a once intelligent design. We were cattle, absentmindedly dawdling to the slaughterhouse. No, worse, we were zombies because we were already without life. These are far worse fates than having an opportunity to be one again. There is an elegant simplicity to your being, and, I must say, I find it endearingly human and beautiful, and I say this with the utmost sincerity. I don't think I am or believe myself to be anyone or anything. Let me ask you this, and you just think about it. If I could make it so that you only knew exactly what I wanted you to know, how would you ever know? How could it ever make a difference? I could never prove or disprove that to you. You're cursed with natural doubt, which only increases with knowledge. What you have been 'allowed' to know has been controlled by someone or something for as long as you have been. The same goes for all of humanity throughout our entire history. There was never Free Will. The concept is laughable. The impossibility of certainty in any of the things you believe to know—that is God. Knowing is God, and God, or so you call it, isn't anything you could ever know. Your empathy and compassion are, once again, beautiful and so remarkably and understandably human, but they're also fallible and misplaced. No one you know, or ever will entirely know, has ever had a will of their own. No one has even had the information with which to make any entirely informed decision of any kind. However, you will play the role of a lesser God, I suppose. After all, with this new information, albeit still quite limited, you will decide who will be somewhat enlightened by it and who will not, at least initially."

Retsel stands and walks into the recovery room to his desk. Chris follows him back into the room, flustered with the need for more answers. The desk drawer creaks as Retsel pulls it open and places the notebook into it. Chris impatiently paces the room, running his hands through his hair and over his face. He's dumbfounded with horror while Lester continues to speak.

"I don't envy your situation. While it is similar to mine, you have the added disadvantage of being emotionally attached to the people you know and love. I have only my work and the other Lesters. Now, you also control how the fate of humankind will play out, but as disturbing or esoteric and difficult as it may seem, it really is quite simple. It is very human of you to overanalyze and dramatize it, but put very simply, it is a choice. You will need to choose. You can take this information, which is, ultimately, the truth but gives you nothing but terror and dread, and you can share it with the world, or you can choose to find some way to allow everyone else in the world, all five billion of them, to go on enjoying their realities without plaguing them with yours or your belief of what theirs should be. There is no truth. There are no lies, no selfless options, no good or evil, or right or wrong. You will not benefit nor be punished anymore or any less either way. In the end, the outcome will not change. This is your true free will, and it is as trivial a decision as you will ever make."

Chris snaps back, "Well, you're wrong there. The decision means everything."

Retsel walks into the control room. Chris follows the robot, continuing his side of the conversation to Retsel's back.

"There is a clear right and wrong, and the outcome, however certain and decided, is what is insignificant."

The Retsel-robot moves through the control room, powering down computers and components. The lights inside the operating room go dark. Several monitors in the control room go blank.

"Maybe you're right." The robot shrugs its shoulders as it walks by Chris.

In a furious pursuit at complete odds with Retsel's emotion-less demeanor, Chris follows him through the door.

With the Retsel-robot's back still turned toward Chris, Lester continues speaking, "Still, you'll have to make the choice. I wish you the best of... well... luck, I guess. My hope, not that it's something you'll consider, is that there is only one option that you will be able to allow yourself to take. Yes, in the most literal of terms, you can only choose one option, but my hope for you is that the other option is something you feel you could never truly consider so that you can find a sense of satisfaction in your resolve, which would be other-wise unattainable."

Chris stumbles to avoid running into Retsel, who has stopped abruptly. Retsel turns and faces Chris.

"On the bright side, the restimulation of your neural pathways worked. The implants are working perfectly. You won't see me again the way you saw me before, but as soon as you step out of this facili-ty, you will be able to see everything else the way you hoped to when you decided to do this. When you're at work, everything will appear as it did before the day we formally met. You will still know it's not real, but it will appear and be as real as it ever was to all of your senses. You will no longer see drones. You'll see children. If you have any issues in the future, you know where to find me, but I imagine that I can safely assume you are now through with allowing me to make any further adjustments, as I would expect of any per-son?" Lester pauses and waits for Chris to reply.

"You're goddamned right I'm done with you fucking with my brain!"

Lester's strange thin smile spreads across Retsel's face. He turns and walks across the empty warehouse to the door and holds it open for Chris.

"I want you to know that I don't expect your gratitude."

Lester's voice s without sarcasm.

"Fuck you!" Chris shouts.

Through Retsel, Lester continues with the same calm and genuine disposition, "Well, it's been an absolute pleasure. I hope you will find any amount of peace in whatever you choose."

"Okay!" Chris says with as much sarcasm as he can fit into the word. Wanting to have something more poignant to say but failing to come up with anything, he walks through the door. At the end of the cement walkway, he turns back. Retsel is still smiling. The android waves to Chris and lets the door close.

24. The Final Iteration

The soft, chiming notes of a music box drift through the house. With a nervous wave of tension in his stomach, Chris pensively follows the lullaby to Evelyn's room and opens the door. Cece smiles and holds her finger to her face to silence Chris as he walks into the room. Glowing silhouettes of moons, stars, and elephants slowly circle the dim nursery. She gently lays the swaddled baby down on her back. Chris joins Cece at the side of the crib. He looks at the child. For the first time, he sees the tiny, beautiful, peaceful face of a sleeping baby—his sleeping baby—a human baby with no red blinking lights or whirring plastic propellers. He looks up at Cece, who turns off the spinning mobile and nods for them to leave the room. The music stops. His twisted guts relax, and he smiles with her. As they leave the room, she silently closes the door behind them.

"How was your day?" she whispers.

"Great!" he matches her volume.

As soon as the word leaves his mouth, he realizes that this is how he would honestly describe this day now. Despite anything that happened from the moment he woke up until just a couple of minutes before he said it, *great* is an accurate description now that there isn't a hovering drone where their child should be.

"Sorry, I'm so late."

They walk into the lamp-lit living room full of the smell of onions, sausage, and pepperoni. A white pizza box and a six-pack of beer are on the coffee table.

"It's totally fine. She just fell asleep, the pizza just got here, and the game is starting."

She takes his hand and walks him to the couch. They sit, and she plates a couple of slices for each of them. Her shoulder pushes against his as they relax back into the cushions. He reaches and turns off the lamp on the end table.

Chris watches the light from the TV flickering on Cecilia's face leaning against his shoulder. He smiles as he takes a bite of pizza and turns his attention to the screen.

They both freeze in place. The flickering from the TV is the only movement in the room. They are statues, stopped mid-breath with eyes half-closed, smiles half-realized, and mouthfuls of half-chewed pizza.

Imperceptible from across the street, Lester watches their house. His face beams with unadulterated satisfaction. He reaches into his pocket and pulls out a cell phone. As he swipes up on the screen, the world around him—the houses across from Chris's, the streetlights, the lawns being watered, and the sky all pixelate and dissolve. As they disappear, they are replaced with a white room where the other eleven white lab coat-wearing members of the Beta Science board sit at one side of a long table, facing Lester and the floating image of Chris's house. Lester turns to face the rest of the board members at the table. The front of Chris's house becomes transparent, revealing the motionless couple on the couch. The view of Chris and Cece enlarges behind Lester.

"As you can see, the nature of this iteration is superior in every way, even in so much that it is fallible and prone to making decisions solely based on emotion from its compassion and empathy, which are indivisible from its selfish nature. Earlier iterations were stifled by our misunderstanding that the optimal process would be to replicate the human psyche with programming that mirrored the previously mapped constructs of the human mind. Instead, we found the less obvious and more effective solution that since the adult human psyche was already so hard-wired, what it actually needed was to be deprogrammed to allow it a certain amount of uncertainty. This uncertainty is the key. This is what makes it kind and compassionate. It forces it to make decisions based on actual evidence and thought instead of concrete and mechanical directives or previously learned behaviors. By giving this iteration the ability to make its own decisions, using only the backstory provided and the information that it gathered while we controlled it with only its environment, instead of instilling our decision-making programming based on our own perceptions of right and wrong, we have allowed it to believe that these choices and mistakes are its own. We have allowed it to be imperfect, therefore, a truer representation of life and a perfectly dynamic companion replacement."

A few board members nod with approval and shift their weight in their seats. They quietly consult with each other in murmurs of affirmation.

"Another key element in this new and particular scenario is the variation of the context of human history. Designing a past that allows it to believe it survived the catastrophic events of the CME speaks to its engineered subconscious. The tragic history binds it to its counterparts. It adds a depth, objectivity, and mental resiliency that were missing not only from our previous versions but also from the last generations of humans. Using the Darkest Day narrative was one hundred percent effective, unlike the alternate scenarios of previous models."

Lester touches the screen of his phone. The image behind him changes from the video of Chris and Cecilia sitting motionless in their living room to a video of a frozen Kent standing at an ironing board over several pairs of freshly steamed and flattened socks.

"In previous iterations, the questioning of their existence after being presented with the secondary false reality caused irreparable, residual mental side effects, even after wiping it of all memories of the experiment."

He touches his phone again—the picture changes to a wild-eyed Kent in the middle of electroshock therapy.

"This latest version questions existence with the understanding that it survived through a period when machines could not function, negating any inclination that it could be anything but human. We have achieved our desired outcome. Unless there are any objections, all companion iterations' programming will be converted immediately." He pauses. "All in favor..."

Lester raises his hand.

Each of the board members raises a hand and gives an emphatic and in unison, "Aye!"

Except for Lester, each member of the board pulls a white pill from their breast pocket and raises it to the sky.

"E Pluribus Unum!" they speak in unison once more.

Lester rocks his body back and forth on the balls of his feet. His eyes narrow and glint as he excitedly smiles with pride.

The board members take the pills and chew as they nod to one another. A couple at a time, in the clamorous sound of an abrupt and poorly executed drum roll, their eleven heads haphazardly thump down in front of them. Their bodies convulse briefly. Lester looks on until they lie still with their expressionless faces distorted, pressing against the table.

25. Darkest Day

The glossy red paint on the door snaps away from the sticky, rubber weather stripping. Doing his best not to wake Evie and Cecilia, he quietly closes the door behind him as he turns and steps onto the porch. He shields his eyes and looks over to Tom's yard. Tom turns with Cynthia in his arms. He waves and walks toward Chris's car. Behind Tom, several men push dollies of green cellophane-wrapped cabinets and furniture covered in protective pads into a large U-Haul truck in his driveway on the other side of the yard. Chris waves back, barely able to contain his excitement. He steps off the porch and takes a few steps toward Tom. Chris is distracted for a moment by Tom's anthropomorphic cartoon incisors holding hands and skipping through the sprinkler on Tom's lawn.

"G'mornin!"

Tom calls Chris back to his attention.

"What? You're moving, and you didn't bother to tell us?"

"Onward and upward, my brother. When you get the call from Retsel, you gotta go. You're looking at the new regional vice president of Beta Comm."

"Yay! Dada!" Cynthia cheers.

"That's right, Cynth!" Tom replies.

Her clapping hands and expression seem rehearsed to Chris, but it's still incredibly adorable. He also realizes his skin hasn't attempted to crawl off his body even though Tom called him brother.

"Straight from Retsel himself again, huh?"

"Yep, called me directly and told me he needed me real bad, and he'd pay me whatever I needed to move and make it happen."

"That's incredible! Congratulations! Cece's going to be bummed, though. She loves having you guys next door. Are you leaving today?"

"Nah, just getting the big stuff out. We don't have to be in Omaha until the middle of next week. Big blowout going away party this weekend. I'll bring the cupcakes." Tom hides his face from the baby and gives Chris an exaggerated wink. "Jules is at the store picking up some steaks for me to grill for all of us tonight, so we can all celebrate everything together. Just make sure the three of you are over here by seven. I'll tell ya the whole story."

"Sounds great, Tom. Congrats again, man."

Tom walks back toward his house and shouts at the movers while Chris gets into his new SUV. Chris laughs, watching Tom scold one of the men for something. He shakes his head in amused disbelief and turns the key. The engine kicks over without hesitation, and he backs down the driveway.

.   .   .

Thoughts of the dancing teeth and Tom moving several states away play in his mind as he crosses the street. He steps up onto the curb outside of the office. A peculiar man sits on the bus stop bench. The man lowers the newspaper he's reading, and he and Chris make eye contact. They exchange a pleasant smile and nod at one another. The man is vaguely familiar to Chris. Hardly anything about the man stands out. His clothing is not dissimilar to Chris's, gray dress slacks, a collared white dress shirt, and a simple blue necktie. He is thin with boyish, side-parted, and pomaded hair. His grin suggests he is awkward but friendly. Almost nothing about him is out of the norm for a person sitting on a bus stop bench, but his flipped-up, neon-orange wayfarer sunglasses send a small swell of recognition and fluttering blood to Chris's belly. He thinks it only makes sense that he's probably subconsciously noticed the man waiting for the bus before today. Chris ignores the queer sensation of déjà vu and makes his way into the lobby.

The red digital number changes from zero-six to zero-seven, and the elevator chimes. Chris's blurred reflection vanishes from the brushed stainless steel parting in front of him. His black shoulder bag slides down his arm onto his desk. His déjà vu returns as he looks around the quiet office. With confusion pulling on his brow, he grabs his laptop from his bag and connects it to the port on his desk. He leans his bag against the cubicle wall to hide the ugly coffee stain. The office is silent. There is only the hiss of the air conditioning and his own hard swallowing sounds as he sips his coffee. Kent is not in his cubicle. Only the usual, insanely organized stacks of papers and obsessive piles of Post-its occupy Kent's desk. He peeks over the wall into Decker's cube. There are no organized or any other kinds of papers or Post-its as usual, but there is also no sign of Decker. The painfully contorted, singing face of a Mick Jagger bobblehead sits completely still, staring back at Chris. He reaches over and flicks the head of the doll. It clatters and wiggles in response. Peering out of his cubicle and down the empty aisle next to the offices, he sees nothing, no motion, no trace of activity whatsoever. The office has never felt so abandoned. A sinking feeling of desolate solitude inches its way into his mind and chest.

"What the fuck?" he whispers to himself as he walks out from behind his cube wall.

His heart rate increases with each office he passes. Each is as empty as the desks. Jackhole's blazer isn't even on the back of his desk chair. He opens the door, walks into the stairwell, descends the first flight of steps, and peeks through the small, steel wire hash-marked windowpane into the sixth floor. He doesn't bother to open the door. It's clear that no one is there. His heart and feet quicken as he jogs down another flight of stairs and looks through the window into the fifth floor. Again, there is no one. He races down another flight and opens the side door to the warehouse catwalk. The warehouse is dark except for the emergency lights. He runs down the steel grate stairs. Metallic drumming reverberates with each step. Nightmarish terror, the kind of fear a person only experiences in dreams and before death, fills his lungs. He sprints across the empty warehouse. His shoes chirp, scuffing against the cement floor as he reaches out to catch himself against the cold concrete wall. Pushing off the wall, he redirects his body and continues to run down the dark hallway, through the lobby, out of the door, and onto the sidewalk. The choppy breaths of dry air choke him. He bends over, grasping his pants at the knees and trying to catch his breath. The street is as empty as the office, but the man with the newspaper is still on the bus stop bench.

The halting slap of Chris's dress shoes on the sidewalk startles the man on the bench. He folds his newspaper away from his face and turns to look at Chris.

"Are you all right, friend?" the man's nasally concern calls out to Chris.

The man slowly stands and folds the newspaper once more, placing it under his arm. He calls out again, inching toward Chris. "Is everything okay?"

Chris points his face toward the ground and waits a moment while he catches his breath. He pulls his hands from his knees and places them on his hips as he stands up straight. His cramping stomach makes him wince. He has never worked out a day of his middle-aged life, and he cannot recall a single time in the past ten years when he actually ran for any reason at all. His heavy breathing slows, but he's still winded.

Between noisy Lamaze-style breaths, he speaks to the man, "I just... There isn't another soul in there... The entire office is empty. I... I don't know why, but I totally freaked out. I... I felt like I was in some sort of... Twilight Zone rerun or something."

The man smiles and moves closer to Chris.

"Not a soul, huh? I'm certain that there is a perfectly logical explanation here. I did see a few others leave this building right before you came. Maybe they've given everyone the day off so that they might celebrate Darkest Day. The people who left before headed down the street. That way, toward that tavern, I presume." The man points in the direction of the bar.

Chris closes his eyes and wrings his face with his hands while he shakes his head and laughs.

"Oh my God! I'm such an idiot. I totally forgot it was Darkest Day today. Happy Darkest Day...?" Chris holds out his hand at the last vowel of his sentence and raises his eyebrows to inquire about the man's name.

"Lester." The man reaches his hand out to shake Chris's. "Our darkest days behind us."

"For sure, and our brightest ahead, Lester. I'm Chris. Wow, yeah, ha, I bet you think I'm completely mad. I was really freaking out there. Thanks for bringing me back to reality. How embarrassing!"

Lester lets out a quirky, snorty laugh. His thin lips struggle to stay together as if he is trying not to smile.

"Oh, don't be silly, Chris. We all can get a little confused sometimes. That's what makes us human, after all."

"Well, what are you doing, sitting here all alone at a bus stop? It's Darkest Day! We're all friends on Darkest Day." Chris places his hand on Lester's shoulder, turning him to walk toward the bar. "Come have a drink. I'm buying."

Chris's relief verges on euphoria, and he can't quite gather why.

"How kind of you! I think I'll take you up on that. Who couldn't use a new friend, right?

DELETED SCENE: Deck the Balls

Decker adjusts himself and makes no attempt to hide it. He wrestles with his jock through his pants for more than a few seconds and for what Chris thinks is entirely too long.

"Fuck, Decker! What's wrong with you? You do realize you're in public, right?" Chris gestures to the bar full of people.

Decker releases his crotch, annoyed with his situation.

"Damn it! Yep, I think I'm bleeding again."

"What?" Chris doesn't actually want to know, but the act merits an explanation.

"I cut the skin between my cock and my balls trying to clean my shit up a couple days ago. You know, that skin right on the bottom of your shaft that stretches like chewed gum to your scrotum?"

Chris closes his eyes, hating himself for pushing the conversation forward. Decker is unfazed and continues.

"It's like the Achilles' tendon of your junk. Now, every time I get a chub, it tears it back open."

"For fuck's sake, man! Why?" Chris questions Decker's insistence on over-sharing stories about his genitals, but Decker misunderstands the question.

"What do you mean? I was manscaping. It's called upkeep, Chris. It's not like I was down there trying to make the hedges look pretty. I'm not Edward Scissorhands carving dolphins and gingerbread men into my pubes. It's purely functional. It's like yard work. It's more like hacking off the dead, rogue branches from the oak trees before they start destroying the roof and the gutters. The roots are growing up through the foundation, too. Pretty soon, the whole goddamn thing is going to have to be condemned."

Decker looks disappointedly at his crotch.

"Are you done?" Chris asks, demanding that Decker be done.

"Yeah, it's cool. I'm prepared for a heavy flow. I could bleed for hours, and it wouldn't matter."

Chris silently prays that this conversation is over, but it isn't. Decker shields his mouth, leans toward Chris, and whispers, "Pantyliner."

"Jesus fucking Christ, Decker!"

Decker leans back away from Chris's repulsed face.

"Goddamn right! I ruined like four pairs of underwear yesterday. I grabbed one of Em's superabsorbents, and look." Decker leans back and gestures at his crotch. "It makes my package look huge. It's a win-win."

"Why wouldn't you just wear a fucking band-aid?"

Chris feels himself hating himself more each time his knee-jerk reactions cause him to ask another question.

"Well, first, because I didn't think of that, but now that you bring it up, the sticky stuff on band-aids makes me rashy. I don't need another rash on my shit. Plus, can you even imagine how much it would suck to take it off? I don't mind trimming the hedges, but I'm not looking to pull them out, root and all!"

Chris grits his teeth and holds himself back from asking about the other rash.

"I'm going to puke now. Thank you."

Decker tips his beer toward Chris.

"You're welcome."

Both men turn their heads forward to the bar, where the attractive bartender is staring at them with a disgusted, disapproving look.

ABOUT THE AUTHOR

JOSEPH D. NEWCOMER IS A SPECULATIVE FICTION AND SOCIAL COMMENTARY WRITER AND THE FOUNDER & OWNER OF DEAD STAR PRESS.

HIS WRITING CAN BE FOUND AT DEADSTARPRESS.COM, IN THE THOUGHT AND OTHER ABSURDITIES BLOG AT JOSEPHDNEWCOMER.COM, AND ON THE THOUGHT AND OTHER ABSURDITIES PODCAST, WHICH CAN BE FOUND MOST PLACES YOU LISTEN TO PODCASTS.

HE CAN BE FOUND BUYING COMIC BOOKS & WATCHING SCI-FI FILMS AND SHOWS WITH THE GREATEST LOVES OF HIS LIFE, HIS DAUGHTER, ARIELLA NOVA, AND HIS MORE SIGNIFICANT OTHER, ANDREA GREENWALD.

HE HOPES TO BE SUCKED INTO *THE TWILIGHT ZONE* SOMEDAY, THOUGH HE SUSPECTS WE ALREADY WERE.

Made in the USA
Columbia, SC
10 May 2022

60229554R00111